by
E Tidning

Applied Divination
Redmond

O-69
Copyright © 2022 Emmy Tidning
ISBN 978-1-959786-00-9

Published by Applied Divination
Edited by Emily Paper
Formatted for print by Applied Divination

This book is a work of fiction. If any part of O-69 resembles the life of a known person, living or dead, then they are and were very lucky, indeed. Bingo!

First printing edition 2022
Applied Divination
www.applieddivination.com

For Sherlock the dog,
who accidentally broke my nose and
rendered me unhireable.

All there was left to do was hide my face and write.

CHAPTER ONE

"I'm getting old, Lola. Even my name is old. My parents may as well have named me Beulah." Emma thrust her body miserably into the microfiber sofa, splaying her arms out in mock distress.

"Hair!" Lola leapt off her seat as though she'd seen a ghost.

This scared Emma enough that she bounced up from her position on the white cushions and spun around.

At the evidence that her grandmother's sofa was safe from Emma's fresh coat of red hair color, Lola pursed her lips and pondered Emma's dilemma. "Your name is not that boring."

Emma rubbed her drying hair and noted a soft pinkish color lingering on her fingers. She sat up properly and was relieved when another thorough scan showed that the sofa was unaffected. Delicately, she piled her damp hair onto her head and crumpled her body into the couch with more care, bringing her feet up and hugging her knees. "Emmaline Soledad is the type of name you'd find on a sixty-year-old Spanish librarian."

"That's highly specific," Lola laughed, checking her own freshly dyed locks for split ends. "You Google yourself too often."

"Well, no one else is *Googling* me, if you know what I mean." Emma pulled her knees even closer to her body and sighed. She felt the tickle of need deep in her belly and she blushed at her own joke, hiding her pink cheeks behind her kneecaps.

Lola rolled her eyes but giggled at the double meaning. flipping her long, now blonder, hair over her shoulder, she turned her attention back to her laptop, opening a search engine.

Emma ogled her best friend's effortless beauty. As Lola's blonde locks poured forward down her collar and over her toweled breasts, Emma pouted into her own chubby legs and adjusted her wayward bra strap. Trying to turn her attention to something else, she reached toward the sofa table where a pile of unfinished work documents taunted her. She glared wistfully at the subject's name on the top file but took very little new information off the page. Human Resource work would have to wait until she wasn't in a bad mood.

As Lola typed her own name into a web browser, she remarked, "I'm having trouble in the relationship department too, you know."

Emma put her feet on the floor to stand up. She tossed the sheet of paper back onto the table, which caused the other documents to fall out of their even stack. The names of all the employees who were being laid off that week glared at her, but she did her best to ignore them. She walked from the sofa to their tiny kitchen space, a move that took fewer than ten steps given the small space the two women occupied. "You're gorgeous," she called back to Lola. "You could walk outside right now and have a pile of men all over you in an instant!" She dumped out that morning's coffee grounds and began rinsing the coffee pot. Sexual frustration ate at her, and she attempted to breath deep to try to push it away.

Lola rolled her eyes and huffed. "Well yes, because I'm in a towel." She frowned at the mess of papers Emma had left on the coffee table.

They'd had this conversation before, so Emma didn't push it. Lola would say that men were afraid of approaching her. That they avoided her because they figured she was taken, or out of their league, or who knows what else. She was right, too. More often than not they both went home alone after a weekend of clubbing.

Emma grimaced, accepting their fate. The fact is that Lola was too pretty, Emma not enough, and so the two best friends remained perpetually single.

"I'm the only Lola Zwanzig in the entire world, I don't know why I bother searching my own name. All I get are various social media accounts, most of which I don't even remember the password to anymore. Does anyone even use Friendster?" Lola closed the laptop and watched Emma remove the coffee filter from the machine. "Should we be having more coffee at six in the afternoon?"

"It's Friday. I figured we were going out to the club again tonight, to show off our new 'dos," Emma pumped her hand up to her hair, dumping the coffee grounds in the trash and rinsing the filter.

Put coffee filters on the shopping list, she said to herself again for the third time that week. *Also, make a shopping list. Also, put said list in an easy-to-find place.* She looked for a pen and paper and noticed the half-empty food containers on the counter.

Lola stood from the table in a thoughtful trance, and moved to the window, staring out at the ugly parking garage across the street.

Emma busied herself throwing out the previous evening's Chinese food, promptly forgetting what she had just told herself to do.

"If you keep doing what you've always done, you'll always get what you've always gotten," Lola mused as she leaned into the window and looked out toward Pioneer Square, the Seattle hipster neighborhood they called home.

"Hmm?" Emma took a bite out of day-old fried rice and wrinkled her nose, but continued munching on it.

Lola pressed her forehead up against the glass, followed by her two hands and perky chest. "We go to the club every night and get the same result," she sighed, and her eyes followed two tourists up the street. "We either never get laid because we're unapproachable, or when we do get laid it's by corporate lawyers who think they're god's gift."

Emma laughed and joined her best friend at the window.

"And I'm getting a bit tired of corporate lawyers," stated Lola firmly, then she began to laugh herself.

Emma followed her friend's gaze into the street toward tourists and hipsters wandering up and around Yesler and 1st streets. She held the fried rice container out and Lola took it unconsciously, eating the contents without moving her eyes from the street. *We really need a shopping list*, Emma told herself again, but made no effort to find a piece of paper. The women watched a group of camera happy people enter a door and descend into the Seattle Underground tour, a popular attraction across the street.

"Let's do something different," Lola continued her thought.

"Do you want to take the underground tour again?" Emma took the rice back from her roommate and dumped the remains down her throat.

Lola bit her lip in thought. "No, let's do something we've never done." She spun around from the window and eyed the living room. Emma followed Lola's gaze around the early 20th century architecture, along the mahogany crown molding and the wrought iron chandelier, memories of a bygone era.

Emma soaked the atmosphere in too, thoroughly confused, but as her best friend was prone to fits of whimsy, she stayed quiet while Lola's mind wandered.

Finally, Lola continued her thought. "My grandmother loved this place. She loved living in Pioneer Square. She loved Seattle. She had such a great life."

"It's a lovely place to leave to you to you and your sister. I'm thankful you let me move in," Emma nodded, as she always did when Lola surveyed her late Grandmother's estate.

Lola wasn't listening. "My grandmother had a wild life, you know." She smiled, not caring if Emma responded or not. "She never married my grandfather."

"Your poor mom was a bastard," Emma stated with a smirk. They'd been best friends since childhood, so Emma knew well that Lola's mom was bitter about having unmarried parents. Lola didn't take after her at all. Emma smiled silently to herself and watched her beautiful friend swing around the room, touching the antique furniture her favorite grandmother had left to her. Emma didn't know where Lola was going with this, but she relished in the vision of her friend's smiling face and dancing body.

"My grandmother was simpler in her old age, of course" Lola paused at the writing desk, not used for writing in twenty years, as computers and internet had taken over both before her grandmother had passed. It especially wasn't useful now, as Lola and Emma took over the apartment with their high tech jobs. "But she still had fun. I would ask her what she was up to on a Friday night, and she'd say the same thing every week..."

Emma eyed her friend suspiciously. If Hetty was like her granddaughter even a little bit, Emma expected a wild story about dancing or the theater.

Lola's response seemed apropos of nothing. "I'm going to Bingo."

Emma's eyebrow shot up. She looked into her empty container of rice as though it knew something she didn't. "Bingo." It was a statement, not a question, as she repeated the word in her head a few times.

"Bingo!"

Emma moved away from the window, through which some tourists were now stumbling up from the underground tour and straight into the conveniently located pub next door. She wondered what the hell had gotten into Lola. For clarification, she reframed the statement. "You want to skip the club tonight and go to Bingo."

Lola danced back over to the window and nodded with enthusiasm.

"As though we're little old ladies," Emma continued, hesitating for a giggle or some sort of indication that Lola was joking. It didn't seem to come. "After I just lamented being an old lady with an old lady name?"

Lola nodded again, smiling.

"I don't even know how to play Bingo," Emma frowned.

Lola's face dropped a bit as she pondered. Emma took that to mean she didn't know how to play bingo, either. Lola jabbed a perfectly manicured finger up to the ceiling and exclaimed, "I think they just call out numbers and you dab them with a Bingo dabber."

"What the hell is a bingo dabber?"

"Who knows!?" Lola squealed, the smile returning to her face. "You see how this is different? It's something we've never done!"

"We're never going to get laid this way," Emma stomped to the kitchen and threw the empty rice container into the trash.

"We already agreed we were probably not going to get laid anyway," Lola pointed out.

An emptiness crawled inside Emma's womb, but she tried to quash it down. If her best friend wanted to play Bingo, Emma knew they'd be playing bingo. She had no argument against it. Another night in the club would just end in a hangover and probably a letdown, whether she got laid or not.

"Okay. Bingo." Emma confirmed her fate quietly and retreated to her bedroom off the kitchen. She heard Lola giggle and skip to her room on the opposite side of the living area.

Emma wandered aimlessly around her bedroom for a moment, wondering what to wear. *What is a bingo outfit, anyway?*

She took off her leopard print bra and looked down at it, realizing she probably wouldn't need anything sexy, so there was no sense suffering in the bra's too-tight underwire. She tossed it on the bed. A comfy sports bra would do, she figured, and grabbed that and her yoga pants off a pile of clothes on the floor. Next up was her sweater from her alma mater, University of Washington, that she normally reserved for hangovers on Saturday morning.

"Go Huskies," she sighed as she pulled the large hoodie over her freshly dyed hair. She grumbled to herself but plastered on a smile and left her room.

Lola was still perky, bouncing around the living room in a sexy tank and short skirt.

"That's what you're wearing?" Emma eyed Lola's cleavage and frowned down at her hoodie. Her chest was almost flat in the sports bra, and made flatter by the sweater, if that were even possible.

"I still want to look good," Lola giggled. "There may be people there who knew Hetty."

"I don't think those people will care one iota about how we look," Emma sighed, as she slipped her feet into some flats and opened the apartment door. "Now let's get on with our wild selves."

CHAPTER TWO

he bingo hall was ten blocks away in a rented space upstairs from a senior center. The women each wore a pair of runners and chose to walk the distance rather than take a Lyft. It was in an area they didn't know well, save for a few pubs they'd frequented in their college days. They almost walked right past the senior center, a set-back entryway the only sign of its existence in this small part of Seattle's First Hill neighborhood. A piece of paper taped to the door indicated that Bingo was around the back of the building.

The journey through a dark alley and up the rear staircase felt like a drug deal gone awry, and Emma stated as much. Lola chuckled and waved an arm at the rest of the clientele entering the building, mostly elderly people and a few college girls dressed in skimpy clothes. "I wonder what drug these people are buying?"

"Luck," Emma laughed. "Just like us."

They took note of the advertising as they climbed the metal stairs and entered the small foyer. It looked like different nonprofit organizations staffed the game and used the profits to fund their missions and programs. This evening's nonprofit was a youth soccer association from south Seattle. A large picture of a boy kicking a dirty soccer ball was taped up on the counter. Emma felt a bit better about the bizarre experience and expenditure. Buying booze at the local pub supported no one but the pub owner, but at least her money would go to charity tonight.

There was a bit of a lineup at the register. They'd expected to find all seniors but were surprised to see a lot of younger women there, too. Further up the line, some twenty-somethings wearing nightclub clothes chortled loudly, perhaps expecting to use their winnings to fund their clubbing later.

Emma and Lola got in line behind two well-dressed, elderly women. One leaned heavily on a charming gold cane, but she peered at the roommates with disdain. Perhaps to her they appeared to be college-aged riffraff, too. Emma's thirty-five-year-old brain hoped so. She smiled and ever-so-slightly bowed, hoping that would impress the woman, but her platitude was met with a huff, and the woman turned to stare ahead of herself again.

As the line moved, they studied the signage and other patrons' purchases, hoping to get some sense of the law of the land before they made an error. Some obvious bingo regulars purchased many packages of cards, and others bought one or two sets only. Lola crossed her arms and pondered, "how many cards do you think we're supposed to buy?"

"I have no idea. One?" Emma shrugged, staring at a display of what she figured were bingo dabbers.

The woman with the cane turned, and in raspy condemnation stated, "you can't buy one card, they come in strips of three cards, nine to a pack. If you've never played, buy the nine-card pack, it's easy."

"I bet I could do eighteen," Lola giggled. "Bingo is in my blood!" The elder woman turned back toward the counter. Emma sensed that she was rolling her eyes at the two of them.

Emma opted for the nine-card starter pack, as suggested, and asked for a pink bingo dabber. The lady at the counter reported that they were called 'daubers,' not 'dabbers,' although she'd forgive the slip for newbies.

Lola bought eighteen cards, a green dauber, and a green-haired troll doll, which appeared to be a popular lucky charm for some of the regulars. They walked beyond the register and into a large hall, eyeing their competition. "Ninety percent female," mused Emma, looking at mostly older women and a few of the younger kids. In a softer voice she ruminated, "No getting laid tonight."

"There's a table with some gentlemen over there," giggled Lola, pointing to the far end of the room, where some very senior men and a couple of women sat laughing at each other's jokes. Emma's eyes rolled, but she smiled. It was possible that one day a ninety-year-old bingo player would be her only chance at love, but she hoped that wouldn't be today.

The younger players were sitting toward the center of the room, and there was plenty of space at their table, but Lola shook her head no as Emma began to walk that way. Instead, she nodded toward seats beside the elderly women they'd stood behind in line. The silver-haired ladies had removed all sorts of lucky charms from their purses - troll dolls, frogs, and multiple-colored daubers. As they completed their display, and other patrons smiled and waved at them, it appeared as though they were permanent fixtures in the bingo hall.

As they approached a wider empty spot, Lola veered toward the elder women instead and whispered to Emma, "we want to be near people who know what the hell is happening. Let's immerse ourselves in the experience."

The elderly women glared at their approach, but swiftly returned their attentions to properly lining up their cards in some sort of order that Emma couldn't fathom. She plopped her cards down on the table and opened her dauber, wondering how it worked. She stamped on the word 'Bingo' across the top of her sheet of cards, but nothing happened. Lola frowned and opened her own dauber to look at the tip, questioningly.

"You have to dab it a few times to get it going," one of the elderly women stated in a smokey voice. Lola and Emma stamped their daubers multiple times.

Lola dabbed repeatedly at the "O" in "Bingo" and winked. "Hey, what am I doing?"

The long plump tube spurted its ooze into the center of the O, and Emma blushed and giggled. The elderly women puzzled at them, stole a glance at each other, then returned to aligning some frog statues.

"Shush," Emma whispered. "No sexy talk."

"You're no fun, love," Lola flirted, just loud enough for a few neighbors to hear. Emma rolled her eyes but flushed even deeper.

#

Two minutes to the start of the game, commotion died down to a quiet lull and patrons began whispering to each other. Emma and Lola looked at each other, wondering what surprises were next.

The numbers on the screen in the front of the room lit up, and a short, graying woman climbed the stage and began spinning a giant cage of balls. Excitement stirred in Emma's belly, but before she could take any new sensory information in, her womb quivered and her face flushed.

What the hell is happening to me, she wondered.

Lola looked up over Emma's shoulder and her eyes widened.

Emma sensed him brush behind her and her body lit on fire. As he passed, she turned and watched a striking figure walk toward the front of the stage. The women sitting in her row smiled after him, waving and even attempting to touch one of his taught muscles. The hunk waved politely at them, patting a few on the shoulder, and Emma saw the muscles in his forearm flex. As he grabbed the handrail to walk up the short stairs to the main stage, she watched his athletic shoulder muscles tighten under his thin polo shirt.

"Where have you been all my life, Bingo?" she said without thinking.

Lola guffawed. "I guess we know why there are so many babes here," she stated simply, watching the sexy bingo caller walk around the ball cage to the microphone.

In a soft but sultry voice, he said, "Hello ladies and gentlemen." As he said 'gentlemen', he looked at the one table in the corner with the older males. Their female compatriots tittered and blushed, which didn't seem to faze their dates. The caller smiled and continued, "thanks for supporting Seattle South Soccer Association. Shall we get started, Mary?"

The short woman smiled brightly at him and spun the ball cage, which rattled and squeaked as the numbers whizzed up a connected tube to the end.

"Damn," winked Emma. "That man is one strong cage of balls."

Lola laughed, and their elderly table mates frowned at the inappropriate joke. Emma was sure she caught them smiling in their cheeks, though. She looked back at the hulking piece of man meat as he continued his intro.

"First ball - B three."

The echo of a hundred daubers thudded against paper on tables, catching Emma off guard. She'd forgotten what she was there to do. Frantically, she scanned her cards for the number. She dabbed at two spots and looked over at Lola, who had about six numbers to hit.

"For those who don't know me," he continued, "I'm Jake. This is the owner and my lovely assistant Mary. "He held a muscled forearm out to introduce his assistant, who smiled shyly and tipped her head. "We're the volunteer callers for the SSSA this weekend, and we thank you kindly for supporting our organization. Fifty percent of the profits from this game go to underprivileged youth so that they can compete in recreational soccer. Another twenty-five percent goes to the senior center events. Next ball is N forty-two."

Once again, Emma was so caught up in listening to him talk, she almost forgot her purpose in the hall and had to force her attentions back to the game.

"Eighteen cards and I don't have any N forty-twos," lamented Lola, and she began dabbing all the free spaces at the center of her cards.

Emma was having so much trouble keeping up with only nine cards, she was wondering how her best friend had scanned eighteen cards so fast. She noted that their elderly tablemates had 27 or 36 cards each and were easily dabbing away as well.

Lola looked up and grimaced toward the young crowd of 20-somethings in the center of the hall. "Look at these ones," she said sarcastically.

Emma watched one of the twenty-somethings stand up and pretend to stretch, but it was obvious she was throwing her chest and cleavage out while she smiled at Jake. He nodded and gave her a pleasant smile back. The young woman scurried around three tables and headed toward the bathroom.

Emma rolled her eyes. "She didn't even have to walk that direction to get to the bathroom."

Lola snickered in agreement. "Now we know why those young kids are here in their sexy outfits." She looked up at Jake with a twinkle in her eye. Emma grew a bit envious of her friend, who looked sexy and provocative in her t-shirt and jeans, and she berated herself for throwing on such a careless and frumpy hoodie.

CHAPTER THREE

T he pace of the game grew faster as more and more people won cheap little games here and there. Emma, flushing with sex at Jake's deep, smooth voice, had trouble keeping up.

Lola was in her zone. "O-seventy-five! I have ten of those!" She tapped her dauber so hard, ink spattered out of it and landed on her troll doll. "Facial!" She laughed, and her eyes were wicked with excitement.

Emma frowned into her card strips. It wasn't that she wasn't enjoying herself, but her mind and her womb were frustrated, and she felt confined in such a small space surrounded by a hundred aging people and the few younger kids. She needed air.

Relief came in the form of an intermission between the tenth and eleventh games. Lola and Emma watched the other patrons abandon their strips and crowd out of the entrance doors, desperate for a cigarette. Emma watched Jake turn off his microphone and whisper something in his assistant's ear.

She nodded and began collecting the small plastic balls, obviously preparing for the later games. Jake leapt off the stage and in a few swift movements of his long, muscular legs, he absconded toward the office room behind the front register.

Four elderly ladies called him back out and chatted with him. He bent down and kissed the hand of one of them, and all of them giggled. Emma's stomach flipped and she jumped up from her chair, half shaking.

Lola looked up from her cards, as if noticing Emma was there for the first time. "Are you getting a drink?"

Emma bumped into her chair as she turned in the direction of the concession stand at the back of the hall. Pulling in a deep breath, she straightened her body in order to get herself together. Out of the corner of her eye she saw Jake leave the smiling ladies and re-enter the small office near the front register.

She sucked in more air to cool herself down. "Drink. Yes, I need a drink. You want something?"

"Looks like you need something a bit stronger than a diet soda." Lola winked at her friend, clearly picking up on Emma's heat.

Emma blushed but composed herself quickly. She snapped, "do you want a soda or not?"

"Yes, please," Lola said sweetly. She refocused her attention on disposing of her used cards and tidying up her space for the next game.

Emma stomped toward the register, sexually frustrated. It was going to be a long second half. She pined for the pub, where she could hook up with a corporate lawyer to get her frustrations out, and then happily ditch him by midnight. Lawyers were just as frustrated and noncommittal as she was.

As she bellied up to the soda stand, an acne-pocked teenaged boy ran up to take her order.

"Hi," she smiled at him. "I'll have two diet cokes."

The kid seemed startled and amazed at her presence, and he looked her up and down appreciatively. She was flattered that at least her hoodie could attract *someone*, even if he was high school jailbait. She attempted to adjust herself to look even less appealing, if that were possible. There was no sense sending the wrong messages to this one, but she did continue to smile.

Hell, she thought, *he might become a corporate lawyer one day.*

"We don't get people as young as you very often," said the boy. "Only on certain days."

"Soccer days?"

"Yes, how did you know?"

"I had a hunch." Emma smirked and looked back toward the front office, but there was no sign of Jake. The boy missed the insinuation and continued to goggle at her. He could obviously comprehend sexual drive at his age, but he probably didn't understand how handsome his competition on stage was.

Emma realized that if the kid didn't comprehend the sexual pull Jake had over his clientele, she may be able to get some details on him. "Tell me about the staff here," she prodded the kid as he filled the drink cups with ice, one cube at a time.

"Bob and Mary work the front desk selling cards. They're the owners. They're also my grandparents," the boy added this last statement with a shrug, as though he was resigned to work for his granny and gramps until the day they died. "The soccer association is the current nonprofit they're supporting, so Jake volunteers here on Fridays and Saturdays, and Grandma Mary works as his ball assistant." The boy's demeanor changed to one of slight melancholy and he added, "Jake was my coach in soccer last year."

Emma tried not to appear too interested. She watched the kid finish topping up the ice, dump part of it back out, and scoop more up again. He repeated this a few times before the cup's ice level appeared to be acceptable to him, then he moved on to the diet coke nozzle. She wanted more information but didn't want to seem pushy.

"What's he like? Jake. What's Jake like?" She immediately regretted her blabbering. *Way to be surreptitious, hot shot.*

The kid did not seem to pick up on her quizzing and answered honestly. "He was awesome, he led our team all the way to the finals." He seemed to say this last part dreamily, spilling the diet coke over the side of the cup. "Shit!" He motioned as though he were going to dump the entire cup all the way out.

Emma reached across the counter and put a hand on his wrist. "It's okay, my friend will take that one."

The boy sighed and nodded a thanks.

Emma could tell by the way he'd counted out the ice that he had some sort of perfectionism disorder. "I'll have mine with no ice," she stated quickly, saving him from another trial with the ice bucket.

"I'm the slowest server here," he said. "I don't know why my grandparents are making me work this weekend. It's our busiest month."

"So, Jake isn't here all the time?" Now that she knew his pull drew the most clientele, she figured she might as well cut to the chase.

"No, just when soccer is the nonprofit. How did you know?"

"Another hunch." Obviously, the kid didn't understand the sex appeal Jake offered the crowd. Changing the topic, she smiled again. "I'm Emmaline." She used her full first name in the hopes that it's old-ageyness might scare the hormonal teen off.

"Aidan," he said, and finished filling the second coke, placing the lids carefully upon them and tapping down all the edges. He seemed frustrated with himself.

Emma handed him five dollars and tried to assure him. "Sometimes perfection is a good trait to have."

"Not in the food service industry," he lamented, then looked over her shoulder and his face lit up.

Emma felt the hairs on the back of her neck rise. Her cheeks burned red with lust. Once again, her body knew Jake was there before her brain did.

"Hey kid," she heard over her shoulder. His voice was even more soothing without the microphone. It was deeper, more daring. She ever-so-slightly shook her head, trying to pull herself together. She clutched at the sodas and turned to move away from him and escape, but she was too late. "Who's your friend?" His voice was directed straight into her ear, and down deep into her belly.

"This is Emmaline." Aidan took the five dollars in the till and began to draw change.

"Emma. Keep it," she said quickly, and attempted once more to turn in the other direction.

His voice set her body ablaze again. "Hi Emma, I'm Jake."

She wrinkled her nose and turned back in his direction but didn't dare look directly at him, lest he pick up on her blushing heat. She attempted to look anywhere but his eyes.

Unfortunately, his eyes weren't his only body part that made her quiver. His chest was taught under his cotton shirt, and his shoulder muscles hugged his collar like he was a bodybuilder. She couldn't find a place on him to look that didn't cause her womb to quake.

She knew she had to say something, so she closed her eyes in a long blink so she could focus on vocabulary. "Hello Jake, nice to meet you." It came out forced, in a bizarre squawk. She winced at herself and fumbled backward, opening her eyes right into his smoky gaze. His irises were like planets of hazel space dust and fire.

She took a deep breath and clutched at the diet sodas as though they were life rafts. The lids popped off and the liquid spilled down her hands. "Oh, shit!"

Jake dove for the napkin dispenser.

"Oh my god," Aidan's voice broke, "I thought I secured those well enough." He stomped and cursed himself.

Emma felt horrible. "No no no, you did, Aidan. Thank you. They were very secure, I'm just a klutz, I should have warned you." She forced a laugh.

Thankfully, Aidan's shoulders relaxed, and he laughed, too.

She put the drinks down and began to secure the lids again.

Just as she thought she'd composed herself enough, she felt Jake's hand on hers drying her off with the napkin. The skin on her arm flushed, and she took a quick breath. The heat was immediate and traveled from her fingers up through her forearms into her shoulders, spreading up her neck and down across her breasts. Her nipples hardened and she felt a wetness grow in her yoga pants.

She stumbled out of his grasp and muttered, "I'd better get back to my friend." She clutched the cups more carefully this time but scrambled to look away from Jake's body as fast as possible.

"You're still dripping," he called after her, obviously confused.

"In more ways than one," she breathed, just out of his earshot.

CHAPTER FOUR

Back at the table, Emma unloaded the sodas with such ferocity she knocked over one of Lola's troll dolls. Her best friend raised an eyebrow and grinned broadly. "So, what's the sexy bingo man like?"

Emma huffed in sexual frustration, every corner of her body wilting rapidly. She attempted to compose herself with a lie. "I don't know, I ran away."

"What's wrong?"

Emma sat in her chair and sighed, slumping her shoulders and bending her forehead down, fretting into the bingo cards in front of her. She took a long sip of the iceless soda, staring into it as though it held the answers.

She both laughed and cried at her misery. "I'll be fine. Something is just wrong with me."

Lola adjusted the fallen troll doll, brushing her fingers through his hair. "Yes, we both know that. By the way, he's still looking at you."

Emma straightened her shoulders, eyes wide. "Did he see me all miserable?" At her best friend's nod, she whispered, "Oh my god, I'm mortified." She didn't dare look over at where she'd left Jake and Aidan. "What do you mean, *still* looking at me?"

"He watched you walk all the way back here." Lola's grin widened across her face, her amusement growing with each of Emma's embarrassing moments. "Whatever you did had an effect on him."

"I did nothing! I stood there like a moron and then when it was time to say something, I spilled coke all over myself."

Lola shrugged and began dabbing her free spaces for the next game. "Ooooh, hot! Some people have weird fetishes; maybe sticky spilled soda is his." She rubbed her bingo dauber like she was giving it a hand job, and gave Emma a broad smile.

Despite her humiliation, Emma laughed. She took a deep breath and dared herself to take one quick look around the hall. Her aim was to pretend she was looking for someone, but she failed. The first place her eyes went when she moved her head was directly into Jake's beautiful hazel irises, still staring into hers as he laughed with Aidan. Butterflies jumped through hoops in her belly, and she smiled back at him despite herself. Not wanting to stare too long, she quickly looked back at her best friend.

Lola winked at her. "Now then, Bingo wasn't such a bad idea, was it?"

"This was a stupid idea and you know it," Emma lied. "But I am enjoying the view."

Patrons started filing back through the heavy doors and shuffling into their seats, carrying with them the faint scent of smoke and bourbon. Emma wondered if it was the elderly gentlemen in the corner who had smuggled in the booze, or if it was the 20-something females. Age had no meaning when it came to sneaking a drink, she figured.

Man, could I use a real drink, she thought to herself.

She took a giant gulp of the diet coke as Lola chirped, "Heads up."

Jake passed behind Emma again, and again she felt the familiar flames of his presence ignite her flesh. Part of her loved the excitement, another part was angry with herself for responding so instinctively, embarrassing herself with blushing goosebumps. Her stomach flipped and she adjusted herself in her chair, trying desperately to move away from him to quell the nervous jitters. She looked over her shoulder as he passed, and he nodded at her.

"Nice meeting you," he smiled. Her blush deepened and she quickly turned away toward her cards.

Jake turned and put a hand on the shoulder of the senior woman sitting beside her, who in turn giggled and patted his arm. Together, the two older women at Lola and Emma's table began to throw gushing comments at him.

"Jake, we're so glad you're back!"

"How's the job, Jake?"

"Are you coaching the boys again this year?"

Jake gave Emma's neighbor another pat on the shoulder and acknowledged this last question with a sad shake of his head. As he put his hand back down on the woman's shoulder, Emma's cheeks flared with envy over the woman's ability to feel his touch. She turned away to stamp her free spaces, quietly scolding herself for being envious of two perfectly normal old ladies.

Jake said something to the women and his voice filled Emma's head with vivid fantasy, but she wasn't able to focus on what he'd said. She assumed it was about soccer, and she attempted to mimic the faces of the other ladies at the table while she furiously avoided his gaze.

He returned to the stage and the ball cage began to spin. Patrons could be heard switching from the old set of bingo cards to the next, tearing sheets apart and mumbling that this was their game, they could feel it. Lola hummed the theme from Chariots of Fire to herself.

Emma remarked, "You're really into this."

B-fifteen was called, and the crowd madly pushed their daubers to paper like a hundred little gunshots going off. Lola painted her cards in color, she had several of the number. "I do like this game. I feel connected to my grandma."

"I like it, too," admitted Emma. It was a ridiculously simple game - stamp numbers until somebody yells 'Bingo' and then move on to the next round. But she had to admit it was a welcome reprieve from another night of probably not getting lucky at the pub. With that thought, her body caught fire again as she heard Jake call N-thirty-two. The rumble of daubers shook the table and reminded her of being pummeled a hundred times by a hard cock. She shivered and winced at herself.

Lola sensed Emma's slight body motion. "I know why you like it," she winked.

Emma blushed. "Stop," she shook her head and frowned. "I'm enjoying the game anyway, on top of the eye candy."

"Wish there was some of that in here for me." Lola surveyed the room, faking a pout but with sparkle in her eyes. She seemed to be having fun despite the lack of sexual prey in the crowd, and her being happy made Emma happy. Perhaps Bingo could be something they did every few months or so, as an alternative to their typical lawyer hunt at the clubs.

Jake called out, "We've got G-fifty-nine here!"

Lola whispered, "I'd take a geriatric fifty-nine in here."

Emma gasped a little too loud, and twenty heads turned to glare at her. Lola innocently dabbed her G-59s, whispering, "Oooh, here's a cute one."

Emma couldn't stop herself, and she laughed out loud. Fewer faces turned, but the ones that did carried furrowed brows and disdain. She was bothering them, but she didn't care, the joke was a silly one.

"Looks like our new guests like the Gs," Jake hummed into the microphone, making Emma's head turn and her body shiver. "So, here's another one, G-fifty." He winked down at her as he passed the ball to his assistant.

The daubers rattled the tables again. Lola grinned. "He likes you."

Emma's cheeks reddened deeper. "He thinks I'm an idiot."

"You *are* an idiot," Lola mused, "but an adorable one."

Emma stamped her last G-50 and set her dauber down, eyeing her sheet for any sign of a pattern that could resemble a bingo win, but seeing nothing. She shrugged her shoulders and stole another glance at Jake, who seemed genuinely happy to be there pulling balls out of a cage and shouting out numbers. It was a job so simple she could barely wrap her corporate mind around it. Her mind fell to thoughts of the mounds of paperwork she had to do back home, mixed with sexual images of the man on stage in front of her.

"I should just try and enjoy the game for what it is," she said to herself, but out loud.

"Mmm?" Lola did not look up; she was too busy stamping I-29. "I *am* enjoying this. I'm getting close to a Bingo!"

Emma realized she'd missed a call, or maybe two, lost in sex fantasies and her human resources paperwork. She shook her head and furiously searched for I-29, scanning the giant light-up screen on the wall for any other numbers she'd missed.

"G fifty-seven" Jake crooned into the microphone, winking at the crowd. Emma got lost in his voice again.

"BINGO!" Lola's screech echoed around the room. A hundred frustrated patrons threw themselves backwards in their chairs and slammed down their daubers, as if they wouldn't need them again in two minutes when the next round started.

Lola clasped her hands in joy as Aidan's grandfather stood from behind the register and shuffled over to verify the numbers on her card. It was a win, he determined, and he reached into his pocket for cash. The prize was a mere twenty dollars but, if Emma didn't know any better, the way Lola bubbled in glee she would have guessed the prize at twenty thousand. Lola was in a zone here, for sure. Emma wondered how to get her own mind in the zone herself.

I need sex, she considered. *I need hot, raw, naked sex.* Her womb oozed wetness as she gazed back up at the only reasonable possibility.

Jake nodded in their direction as everyone prepped their cards for the next game. Emma pulled her hoodie over her head. Lola smiled and rubbed her troll doll, not noticing the heat Emma was sure radiated from her body.

Emma hoped her drink would cool her down, but as she slurped at it, she remembered telling Aidan hers didn't need ice. She immediately regretted keeping the iceless drink for herself and she clambered at Lola's drink instead.

Lola eyed her questioningly. "What's wrong with your soda?"

"It's not cold enough." Emma hoped this would be enough information for her friend.

It wasn't. Lola continued to stare at Emma, her chin tilted sideways. "Something is wrong with you. You normally dislike really cold drinks."

"I've changed."

Jake's voice hummed into the microphone again, "Game thirteen, ladies and gents. Get ready for some balls."

The crowd tittered; Emma guzzled the drink.

Lola's eyes twinkled and she looked up toward the stage. "You really like this guy. If I had to take a guess, I'd say you were in heat."

"This happens when I'm ovulating," said Emma quickly. "Anyone could make me horny at the right time of the month. Even those guys." She waved in the direction of the older gentlemen in the corner. The woman beside her huffed, clearly disliking their dirty conversation. Emma had almost forgotten they were there.

Lola smiled, but she wasn't buying what Emma was saying. "I've never seen you quite like this."

"Normally we're at a club picking up lawyers, and you can't see me in the dark." She guzzled more of Lola's diet soda, trying to hide her pink cheeks.

"No, this is a real crush. You have a crush!" This last part was squealed a little too loud, and the women next to them stared.

Emma sank down in her seat. *How many people heard that? Had Jake?* She dared not look.

"I mean she's crushed," Lola quickly lied to the elder women, obviously also embarrassed about her loud slip. "She's crushed that I won and she didn't."

"We all are," said the woman sitting next to Lola. "Now shush while the game is on."

Lola shut her mouth, but she winked again at Emma.

CHAPTER FIVE

*W*e're here for fun, Emma repeated to herself as the games rolled on. *I'll do my best to stop thinking about Jake and sex.*

Toward the end of the second half, she did start to have fun, even winning a small five-dollar prize. It was not enough to pay for the evening's activity, but it did cover another round of diet sodas.

The woman sitting beside Lola won a fairly substantial two-hundred-dollar prize, making her a bit cheerier to be around. As the elderly women loosened up, they even gave some helpful pointers to Lola and Emma, such as stacking their card strips in order and color-coding their daubers with their games.

The final game dwindled down to a heated brawl between the table of older gentlemen in the corner and the 20-somethings in the center of the room. One person from each set was only one number away from a full card and the thousand-dollar grand prize. Jake sped up the balls but slowed down his call, in order to raise excitement. The gentlemen tried to remain passive as though they didn't care. The 20-somethings oohed and aahed in anticipation, fluttering their eyes at Jake as though he had control over which ball would come next.

"G is the next ball up," he purred into the microphone. "G fif-" He'd pause for the crowd, and they'd begin to murmur. "-ty-four. G fifty-four."

The fake-stretching 20-something girl fell back in her chair, depressed. That wasn't her number. Lola stamped her G-54s furiously but was still at least three numbers away on most of her cards. The older men were a little slower to stamp, but they didn't win, either.

Emma blew out a breath she hadn't realized she'd been holding onto, and wondered if it was out of anticipation or lust. As she listened to Jake's slow anticipating speech, once again she found herself wishing he'd speak into her neck the way his lips breathed into the microphone. Her body grew hot with lust for him. She'd given up on her cards a few numbers back, stopping to watch him grab those balls.

Another one rolled into the ball trap and he clasped it in his palm. She watched his forearm muscles flex as he brought it into his sight. "Oh," he whispered into the microphone, scanning the crowd with his eyes.

"Ohhh?" Emma sighed, mirroring his mouth with hers.

He seemed to sense her watching him and turned to her. With a smile he whispered audibly "Oh sixty-nine."

She blushed and breathed out air. Oh sixty nine. Ohhhh sixty-nine. Oh, how she wanted to sixty-nine with him right now. On the floor, naked, their muscled legs entwined around each other's heads. She wouldn't care who was watching, she just wanted all of him.

"BINGO!!"

Emma's body shook, and she quickly removed her hand from a breast, not even realizing she'd put it there. She looked toward the table of 20-somethings. One of them was waving her card in the air, tits bouncing, squealing in delight.

Lola grumbled and capped her dauber. Emma gawked at the table, still trying to get her head together. She looked up toward Jake, but he was focused on the lightboard as he helped Bob match up the numbers on the winning girl's card. She'd definitely won the big money.

Emma's sexy moment was gone.

Players grumbled, tossed their cards into the garbage cans, and made their way toward the exit, some of them sticking cigarettes in their mouth before they'd even got up from their chairs. Lola began packing her troll dolls into her small Prada handbag.

"That's it? It's over?" Emma sat upright in her chair, watching everyone amble out of the room. She scanned the stage for Jake, but he'd already left and retreated into the office. She watched women stop by the door on their way out and wave through the small office window, all in flirtatious attempts to get his attention. Emma shook her head, waking herself up from the daze she'd fallen into somewhere between O-69 and the dissipating crowd.

"That's bingo, I guess." Lola scrunched her bingo cards into a ball and pitched them over her table neighbor's head, landing directly into the trash can. Both elder women turned and scowled at her but continued packing up their myriad belongings. "Swoosh," Lola grinned at the woman as she stood from her chair. To Emma she winked, "Well, that was fun, wasn't it?"

Was it? Emma wondered. Could she stand another two to three hours of that if she weren't swooning over the host? She wasn't quite sure, but she nodded and stood from her chair as well, opting to collect her cards more maturely and walk them to the trash can. Her elder neighbor seemed appreciative of her quiet courtesy, or perhaps that was just an assumption on Emma's part.

As they left the large hall and passed by the front office, Emma stole a peek through the door. Jake appeared to be in a deep conversation with Aidan's grandmother Mary, and he didn't show any signs of looking up. Emma didn't want to seem like one of his other stalkers, so she paced quickly toward the exit door.

"You're smitten," Lola reached for the door handle ahead of one of the older men from the corner table. He dragged an oxygen tank behind him and smiled at her keenly as she held the door for him.

"Am not." Emma slowed her pace and followed behind the man.

Jake's voice called from the office door, "Hey, wait up!"

Lola pretended not to hear Jake. She pushed passed Emma and followed the old man out of the building, under the pretense of helping him down the stairs with his oxygen tank. As the glass door closed behind her tight butt, she turned and winked, a clear hint that she was giving Emma a minute alone with Jake.

Emma fumed at Lola but blushed demurely at the same time, wondering how opposing emotions like that were even possible. She watched Lola leave and felt her body warm up with need and anticipation.

"Emma, right? We never got to finish our conversation at the bar."

What she wanted to say was: "Some bar, I can't even buy a tequila" in a sarcastic tone. Instead, what came out was "Soda."

She mentally chided herself and turned her gaze from the door to his legs. She couldn't look him in his steamy, dreamy eyes. She knew she'd orgasm right there if she did.

But his legs, oh god those legs. She tried to ogle his entire lower body without making it evident that she was doing so, but she failed miserably. Her knees began to weaken. She didn't have much time to make an impression. Thankfully there was no soda to spill this time.

"That was fun," she said. Then, realizing that her words could mean a myriad of things, she waved toward the hall. "Bingo. Bingo is fun."

Idiot, she berated herself again.

Jake switched his balance from one foot to the other, and the muscle flex in his legs was evident enough to light Emma's body completely on fire. She could barely process her other senses, the sight of his quadriceps usurped all of her brainpower.

Jake said something.

"Huh," was all she could get out.

"It's just that we don't get a lot of new people. I wanted to give you two a proper welcome and say that I hope you'll come back and support the soccer club this month." Jake waved at a poster of a happy child scoring a goal.

Emma attempted to retrace his words so she could piece together what he was saying. She hoped she could formulate a coherent response. "Right, club. Yes, we'll come back. Bingo is fun."

She mentally admonished herself again. *Why do I sound like a moron?*

"Yeah, anyway, it was really nice to meet you, Emmaline." His voice deepened at her name.

She'd never heard her name said like that before, as though he were reciting a Shakespearean sonnet. Her heart melted. She began to feel dizzy and grabbed the metal door handle to steady herself.

Jake nodded and took a step to retreat toward the office, assuming her slight faint at the door was a hint that she was leaving.

No! Her entire body screamed, but the moment had passed. It was time to go.

She thought quickly, "When do we come back," she said.

What a stupid thing to say.

She coughed and restated her thought. "I mean, when will you or the soccer club be here again? The soccer club, yeah." She was a blubbering idiot at this point.

Dumbass.

"I'll be here tomorrow night." Jake backed toward the office. Then, almost whispering to himself he added, "It's my last day."

"I'll see you tomorrow," Emma replied, robotically.

No, wait, stop being so eager! But it was too late to try and figure out a self-correction. He'd retreated and Aidan's grandparents were already shutting the lights off in the main hall.

Jake smiled and saluted her loosely before heading back into the office.

Emma departed the building at a run and descended the aluminum staircase, grateful for the biting cold outside to chill her flesh.

Lola waited for her at the bottom of the stairs. As Emma stumbled down the last few steps, her best friend smiled and gestured up to the Bingo parlor. "Well, I know you didn't much enjoy it, but I thought bingo was kind of a hoot. We don't have to do it again."

"Quite the contrary," stated Emma flatly, as she passed Lola and turned toward 9th Avenue. "We're coming back again tomorrow night."

CHAPTER SIX

Jake dug his fingers into the tender flesh of her thighs and pummeled into her so hard she couldn't breathe. Her flesh ached in agony for him, her skin lighting up in the flames of passion. He moaned her name as he thrust his hard cock into her wet oracle again and again. As she neared climax his name screeched from her throat and sweat broke out over her burning flesh. Just as she was about to attain the pinnacle of ecstasy, a clown waddled into the cineplex and asked where the birthday party was.

Emma woke in a miserable fury, her forehead damp with the exhaustion of incompleteness. It took her a minute to figure out where she was and what was happening. Her queen mattress, once an opulent sleeping venue for an independent woman, felt vast and empty in the cold Saturday morning. She crawled out of bed, painfully horny and wanting, and fumbled for the bedroom doorknob.

Lola hummed into the coffee machine. "Rough night? I heard you mumbling in your sleep."

Emma wondered exactly how much was heard but, as she preferred to just forget the dream altogether, she didn't ask. She got the coffee out of the cabinet while Lola emptied the filter to reuse again. "We forgot to buy filters again yesterday."

"We were too busy Bingoing. Let's go out this morning. We should probably stock this place up. We're out of Chinese leftovers, too." Emma opened the fridge and frowned into the vast array of half empty condiment jars. "We need to eat better. I have to lose some weight."

"No, you don't, you're perfect."

"No, *you're* perfect. I'm about 30 pounds away from perfect."

"We can't both be perfect," Lola teased. "Plus, you know the song. 'Boys like a little more booty to hold them tight.'" She sang the last sentence off-key, shaking her curves. She returned her attention to the coffee machine. "If anything, I should *gain* some weight."

"Great, you do that. Let's be fat and lonely together here forever," Emma muttered this as she peered condescendingly into an empty milk carton.

Lola frowned. "What the hell is wrong with you today? Do you not like living with me anymore? May I remind you that rent is almost fucking free and you're a god damn millionaire because of it?"

Emma threw the milk carton into the trash and mentally shook herself out of her stupor. She was being a grumpy bitch and she knew it. "I'm sorry. I woke up on the wrong side of the bed. I love living with you."

Lola started the coffee machine and stomped into the living room. The machine buzzed and whirred unusually loudly, and Emma stepped over to it to see what was happening. As she approached it, the lid popped up and the canister crashed to the ground. The machine began spitting hot water and coffee everywhere, including into Emma's chest and down her leg. "Shit!"

Lola ran back from the living room and pulled the plug out of the wall. Emma yanked her t-shirt away from her body to get the heat off of her flesh, and she danced into the living room. "Forget filters, we need a new coffee machine." She stamped her feet down in frustration, shaking her shirt out in front of her breasts.

Lola looked to the ceiling. "Sorry about your coffee machine, Grandma. Maybe tonight we'll be Bingo winners and we can buy a new machine."

Bingo. Ugh. Emma quit shaking her shirt and looked down at herself. She was chubby, sexually frustrated and her only skill seemed to be spilling liquids on herself. How would she survive another night near handsome and smooth-talking Jake? She slouched her shoulders and sighed.

Lola noticed the movement and approached Emma, patting her on the back. "Hey, it'll come out. Go throw some clothes on and we'll go for a walk to Starbucks."

Emma was glad Lola thought she was upset about the shirt and not the real problem, which was her sexual frustration and lust for the bingo caller. She smiled at Lola and observed the mess in the kitchen. Together they bent down to wipe up the coffee and dispose of the machine, Emma taking the liquid on the floor, and Lola breaking up the coffee machine parts and throwing them out. It was almost automatic, Emma thought to herself, the way they each just took a chore without talking. She loved her roommate and best friend, but because she did, something nagged at her.

"Babe," she broached, tossing a coffee-stained paper towel in the bin.

Lola merely hummed as she poured the rest of the hot water down the sink.

Emma continued, "I can't believe how long we've lived here together."

Lola smiled. "I was so glad you moved in with me after the Peter incident," referring to her ex-husband, who'd turned out to be a bit of a gold digger.

"I needed you too," Emma admitted. She'd moved in with Lola shortly after losing an apartment to a condo developer.

Lola slouched. "But you don't need me anymore?"

"No. No no," Emma leapt to her feet and hugged her friend. "Quite the contrary. I need you to show me a world outside software development and clubbing with lawyers. I just wonder if this is where we'll be next year or in ten years."

"I hope not, but would it be so bad? Why is this coming up now?" Lola shrugged off Emma's embrace and wiped coffee off the countertop. "Do you want to move out?"

"I just thought, eventually--"

"We'll get there if we get there. I like living with you."

"I love living with you. But we're in our thirties." Emma sighed and glared out the window, as though searching for time she didn't have any more.

"Oh, I'm sorry." Lola laughed, "I didn't notice when you'd changed from Emma to my Mother." When Emma forced a smile, Lola continued, "I'm happy. I like living in my grandmother's old apartment with someone who knew and respected her. Peter didn't, and now that Hetty's been dead nearly nine years, I don't think I'll find another man who does and is willing to live in an apartment filled with her stuff. Nor do I believe I'll find one who is as tolerant of my obsessive attachment to her."

Emma smiled at Hetty's old apartment—now it belonged to Lola and her sister, Kier. It was still filled with all Hetty's baubles and tchotchkes that the girls used to admire and wonder about in their youth. The only new things were articles Lola had to replace over the years, such as the beds, a table, and now the coffee machine. Emma felt regret over not having properly cared for those things, but Lola didn't seem bothered.

"Look babe, if you one day need to move out, I'll make it work." Lola brought Emma's attention back to the task at hand by handing her more paper towels. "But you're my best friend and I love you, and I'd like you to stay until then. I will never be in a rush to kick you out."

"Unless your dream guy-who-knew-Hetty comes into your life."

Lola's eyes sparkled. "Yes, unless that happens. For now, let's keep banging the corporate lawyers. Just not tonight."

Oh right. Bingo, thought Emma again. She wiped up the rest of the coffee and stood. "I think I'll jump in the shower." *A very long, cold shower.* "And then let's go grab that coffee and hit up Westlake Center. Our next coffee machine is on me, and it'll be a good one." She turned toward the old machine in the trash can. "I'll make you proud, Hetty!"

CHAPTER SEVEN

lmost eight hours later, they stumbled laughing into the apartment, clutching a myriad of grocery bags. A Lyft driver ambled in after them, carrying their gourmet coffee machine.

"Thanks so much!" Emma tipped the driver an extra fifty bucks on top of his pay. He deserved it, he'd been their escort since the coffee machine purchase, the two women not having a way to carry grocery bags along with the large, vintage machine. The driver muttered his thanks and bailed quickly, as though afraid they'd ask him to help set it up.

"Well, now we have food." Emma pointed out the obvious as she shut the door. "We have no excuse not to make ourselves a healthy meal instead of going out for Chinese food again."

Lola left the bags on the floor and dove into setting up the coffee machine, obviously eager to replace her grandmother's broken one and try to move on. Emma left her to it and began emptying out the bags, excited to finally have food to fill the empty spaces between condiment bottles. She started trying to think up easy meals she could throw together, so the two of them could dine in and watch movies all evening. It would be a perfect, quiet Saturday night.

"But if we walk up to that Chinese food place on First Hill," Lola suggested, "we can eat a nice dinner right across from Bingo."

"Ugh, Bingo." Emma frowned into a half jar of strawberry jelly, wondering whether to toss it or keep it.

"You don't want to go?" Lola looked up from the coffee machine manual. "I thought we had fun. You promised Jake we'd be there."

"Jake doesn't know me from anyone else. He wouldn't miss us."

"It's for charity, Em. I was really getting to know my grandma's favorite game."

Lola's pout softened Emma's resolve. She turned up a corner of her mouth and sighed. "For you, babe, anything. Let me shower again, and-"

"-find something sexy? You can look in my closet." Lola continued setting up the new coffee machine with a sly look on her face.

Emma was about to refuse the offer but realized her wardrobe could definitely use the help. She had to make a better impression than that Huskies hoodie she'd worn the night before. If she was going to try for a hookup with Jake, she needed to squeeze her body in all the right places and disguise all the wrong ones. Rather than argue with her best friend, she opted to take the offer of free clothes, and ran to the bathroom to shower and shave—well-- everything.

#

Noting her genetic flare for the game, Lillian and Mabel, the elder women from the night before, began to warm to Lola. They even offered her tips on how to align her cards to get the fastest dab. Emma was slower to get into their good graces, shuffling in apathy at some of the games, and only haphazardly dabbing at her cards. Winning would be difficult on a Saturday, given that the crowd was quite a bit bigger and the pros all had far more cards than she'd ever dare to buy. She spent most of her time ogling Jake as the ball numbers rolled out of his deep voice.

"He's single, you know," Mabel muttered under her breath after Emma emanated a particularly loud sigh at Jake whispering G-53.

"Huh?" She snapped out of it quickly, and noted her table companions all smiling at her, even Lola had joined in the admonishing grin.

"Jake hasn't had a girlfriend since his divorce," Lillian said, and Mabel gave her a look. Lillian coughed and shifted in her chair. "I mean, he's definitely single for sure. Mary says so."

Emma capped her dauber and stood from her chair. She needed a break and tired of her hormones and body giving her away. Mabel pulled Emma's cards toward herself and began dabbing some of the numbers she'd missed. Emma went to the snack bar for a drink and encountered Aidan again.

"Aidan, nice to see you! I'll have two sodas, no ice." She mentally patted herself on the back for remembering the boy's perfectionism problem. It was a wonder she could focus on anything in this bingo hall.

Aidan grinned at her cleavage then caught himself and moved his gaze to her eyes. "My grandparents put me to work on days when Jake is here," he told her. He fidgeted with a stack of cups until he seemingly found two he liked, then put one under the drink machine.

"He's your soccer coach, I take it?"

"He was," Jake said, "he was my favorite coach. We won almost every game of the last season."

"Oh, why did you quit?"

"I didn't," Aidan finished one cup and checked it for fullness. Not quite happy with the amount in the cup, he pushed it up against the dispensing lever quickly for another drop, and another, and another, until it was just right. Then he started the second cup with intense focus.

Emma decided not to distract him further and turned to watch the end of the current game. As Jake purred N-33 into the microphone, Mabel waved her hand in the air and screamed "bingo!"

The bingo checker ran to her side, and the crowd began murmuring and throwing out their first half of cards. Some even got up to rush out for a cigarette before Mabel's win was confirmed. Ultimately, the win was good and Emma watched the checker count out eighty dollars into Mabel's hands. Emma returned her attention to Aidan, who had finished the sodas and was trying desperately not to look at her cleavage.

She pretended not to notice. "How much do I owe you?"

"Uh," he flickered his eyes from her shoulder to her face, back down to her chest, and then toward the cash register beside him. Then he remembered to punch in the numbers. "Four fifty. I mean, four fifty please."

"But half of it goes to the charity, so do leave a tip," she heard Jake's sexy voice from about twenty feet behind her, and she clutched the counter trying to hide her ecstasy. Her nipples hardened, an involuntary body movement that even Aidan noted, his own body probably doing its own thing. She immediately felt responsible for the lad, threw a five on the counter and grabbed each drink in one hand, whipping around with them directly in front of her breasts so as to hide her nips from the rest of the crowd. She made a mental note to always wear a padded bra near handsome men. "I'm so glad you could make it back," Jake approached her and seemed to fiddle with his hands before opting to rest the left one on his hip. He used the other one to signal to Aidan that he needed a soda. "Hit me with a hard Sprite, kid. It's a busy night."

Aidan laughed but hid well behind the counter, and his voice was more high-pitched than Emma had ever heard it. "We only have regular Sprite, Coach."

"Still no booze after years of bugging your grandparents," Jake shook his head. "Oh well."

Determined not to squeeze the juice out of her drinks this time, Emma attempted to compose her heated frame and excuse herself to deliver Lola's coke. Jake caught her arm as she sidled past him, and the shock of his touch sent her nerves reeling. He let go just as quickly as he'd grabbed her, and she felt instant despair. She wanted those muscles on her all the time. "I'm just bringing Lola her coke," she muttered quickly, unable to look at any part of his sexy form.

"Oh yeah, of course. Sorry," Jake seemed entirely too awkward for such a handsome person, as though he'd made a terrible mistake. Emma regretted leaving him, but wasn't quite sure where they could go from here, what with two giant cokes in her hands and a body about to sweat through her thin cotton dress. She scrambled away as quickly as possible while still trying to maintain a sexy swagger. She probably looked like a sick penguin, she thought to herself as she threw the coke cups down on the table in front of her friend.

Lola looked up from her daubers, which she had methodically capped for the second half of the game. "Thanks, what took you so long?"

"Jake stopped me," Emma huffed out in a long, frustrated scowl.

Lola smiled "and why didn't you stop him back?"

"I had your soda!" then, catching herself being angry and frustrated for no reason but her sexual need, Emma softened her voice, "and mine too, I guess."

Lola looked toward the counter and Emma followed her gaze, noting that Jake and Aidan were still gawking in their direction. "Well," her best friend smiled, "you don't have my coke now."

Emma heard Mabel and Lillian giggle behind her, willing her to go back and talk to Jake. From behind her, Lillian whispered "there is still ten minutes before the next round."

Mabel smiled at her friend "enough for a cigarette."

Lola grinned "enough for something."

Emma huffed at their innuendo and retreated from the table, returning back toward the counter. As she approached, however, she scrambled quickly to come up with some reason to return. Forgotten change? No, she'd distinctly left the fifty cents as a tip for Aidan. Lost an earring? No, she wasn't wearing any. More steps, she was getting closer. *Damn woman, think of some reason to be back here.*

As it turned out, she didn't need an excuse at all. Jake grabbed his Sprite from Aidan, took a step toward Emma and gently took her hand as she approached, guiding her away from the counter and toward the office in the front. "Good, you're back, I want to show you something," he said.

Emma didn't bother saying anything, she was done thinking and she was hot as hell. She all but ran ahead of Jake, letting his hand drop from hers. She pulled him by the arm into the front office, where she threw him in first and locked the door behind her. "What did you want to show me," she breathed.

He thrust her body upwards and threw her against the door, pinning his mouth on hers. She coiled her hands around the back of his head and her legs around his hips, as he lifted her from the door onto the wooden desk, using one free arm to push paperwork onto the floor and out of her way. As her ass hit the table he let go and used the other hand to fidget with a desk drawer. She kept her legs wrapped around his torso and bit at his neck, as he fumbled for a condom and she pulled open his jeans. The way his pants leapt away from his body told her all she needed to know about the size of his manhood, and her body grew hotter in anticipation. He sheathed his erection in seconds and didn't even wait for a signal from her, he dug deep into her hot wet box and slammed her hard. She gasped, ready to scream, but he grabbed her mouth with his hand and looked deep into her eyes with the message "the walls are thin." She bit him instead, which caused him to recoil and slam that much harder into her sex again and again, making her wince and weep in his beautiful agony.

As she approached orgasm, she squeezed his cock with her muscles and made him grunt silently, causing him to speed up his pummeling, digging her ass further into the desk. The pain of elation became so unbearable a cold sweat formed on her temples as she tried desperately not to scream. She watched him and could tell he was having trouble staying silent, too. Finally he took her mouth in his as he shuddered with her in simultaneous orgasm.

For about thirty seconds he lay half on top of her, half of him still standing on the floor, as they both came down from the high, trying to slow their breathing while they chuckled into each other like teenagers. Finally, she purred, "Now, what was that about?"

As he withdrew from her body he laughed, "I was about to ask you the same thing." She groaned at the emptiness he left behind but did her best to scramble off the desk and land on her feet. Jake helped her down and looked up at the clock. "I have about sixty seconds to get back up there. I'm sorry that wasn't slower and more romantic." His face seemed miserable and apologetic.

Emma shrugged, trying to ease his mind. It really was not a big deal. Obviously, they both needed the release. She brushed him off with a wave of her hand and told him to go on. She leaned over to look around for her panties.

Jake fumbled awkwardly, staring at the clock but also trying to help her up. "I'm sorry," he said again.

"Please, don't be." She smiled genuinely and shooed him off again. He gave her one last sorrowful glance and sped out the door. She wondered what he was so apologetic for. She could be a sexual camel and was good for another six months now, at least. It had been quick, but oh so amazing. Thinking about him inside her sent another shiver down her spine, and she straightened her dress to make herself look decent again before venturing back out into the hall.

CHAPTER EIGHT

Emma slid out of the office as quietly as possible, trying to let Jake do his thing without being noticed. There were a few sidelong glances, she noted as she walked out into the hall. She hoped they she was imagining the looks as she hustled quietly back to her table. Mabel and Lola each eyed her with one eyebrow raised but said nothing.

Lillian had no such decency. "What'd you see in Jake's office, honey? Does he have a lot of dabbers in there?" She winked and tittered at herself. Mabel giggled but said nothing.

"Nothing happened," Emma lied.

A collective uh-huh hummed around the table, but the ladies happily stamped i-25, the second number called after break. It appeared Jake had gotten his wits about him rather quickly, and was doing his customary flirt with the microphone. Emma tried not to blush, and she wondered to herself how often he took guests into his office at break.

"Do you want your sheets back?"

"Huh," Emma caught herself frowning at the table of younger looking females, and tried to hide her curiosity as to whether they'd also slept with Jake or not.

She didn't care, she really didn't care, at least that's what she told herself.

Mabel cleared her throat and spoke again "your cards, do you want your sheet of cards back? You know, to play the game?"

Emma looked down at the table, where Mabel was playing her nine cards plus twenty-seven others. She felt instant guilt. "Oh yes, I'm so sorry. Thank you for playing for me."

"Here you go, dear." Mabel slid them over. Four twenty-dollar bills were on top of the sheet.

"What's this?" Emma picked up the twenties and tried to hand them back.

"They're your winnings," Mabel stamped G-46, the next number called. "You were getting sodas before the break, and your card won."

Lola berated her "See what happens when you don't play?"

Puzzled, Emma looked down at the eighty dollars for a moment, trying to shake off a post-sex confusion. She took a quick look at her sheet and noted a lack of G-46 on all nine cards, then she dealt out twenty dollars to each of her table mates. First to Mabel, then Lillian, then Lola. The last one she shoved in her bra.

Lillian motioned to push the money back. "Don't be silly, dear, we just played the cards. You bought them."

Mabel shot Lillian a look that said, "don't mess with this, we're on a pension."

Emma smiled. "Seems you guys are doing all my work for me. Plus, this gets me almost all my money back, so I'm playing for free now." She grabbed her green dauber and prepared to stamp the next ball. She wouldn't take no for an answer. The other ladies happily stuffed their twenties into their bags and thanked her politely.

Mabel muttered into her cards. "I hope this totsy doesn't expect us to share the grand prize with her," and the table of women erupted into laughter.

#

In the end, nobody at their table won much more, save for Lillian who stamped four corners and won a free yellow dauber. She gave the dauber to Lola as the shade was too light for her elderly eyes to discern. According to Mabel, yellows were always given away for free as 'prizes' because the bingo hall rarely sold them.

After the final prize was dished out to a dapper octogenarian male in the corner, the women scrunched up their cards and chucked them into the trash bin, all fairly happy to have come away with something. Emma thanked them again for playing her cards while she was away. She blushed again as the memory of sex returned and her skin began to heat up, but she tucked her face into her purse pretending to look for something. If the elderly women noticed the hormonal shift, they didn't mention it. Mabel laughed, "Hey, if you're buying the cards and sharing the prizes, I'm happy to play 'em!"

Lillian retrieved Mabel's walker from beside the table, and helped her friend stand up.

Lola packed up the rest of her expanding dauber collection. "It's ten o'clock, Em, are we heading home?"

Emma was barely listening. Her focus had returned to Jake, who was helping Mary pack up the microphone and return the balls to the cage. She sighed heavily, unaware of her surroundings.

"Or do you want to chill out here some more?" Lola put a hand on her hip and raised an eyebrow.

Emma snapped to attention and felt her friend's gaze on her flesh. She flushed wickedly but faked a nonchalance with a rigid shrug of her shoulders. She realized she'd only heard part of the conversation and didn't know quite how to respond.

Mabel saved her from answering. "I know who you are," she said to Lola, ignoring the one-sided discussion the roommates were having. "You're Hetty's kid."

At the name of her grandmother, Lola's face brightened. "You knew my grandmother?"

"She spoke about you all the time, dear. Used to sit right in that spot with Lillian and myself and make flirty eyes at the table of men in the corner." Mabel flipped her fingers in the direction of the octogenarian who'd won the thousand-dollar prize. A younger man, perhaps in his fifties, helped him up from his seat.

Lola barely registered the men, but stared agog at Mabel, obviously elated that these slightly crotchety old women might know her grandmother. As the women began to shuffle away from the table, Lola spoke, "I want to know more."

Mabel signaled with her chin to follow, and Lola skipped around the table, madly collecting the rest of her things, as though it wasn't obvious that Mabel and Lillian would give her plenty of time. "Walk me to the senior's center next door. I have loads of pictures of the three of us."

Lola shot Emma an excited and nervous look. "Do you mind?"

"I'll come find you," Emma waved her off. "-and I'll clean up the rest of your things here."

Lillian toddled off, and Lola helped Mabel round the tables toward the front door, anxiously peppering her with questions about her grandmother. Emma opened her small clutch and attempted to stuff a few of the daubers and trolls into it, but barely succeeding. Finally, she bent her arm and tucked the remaining pieces between her elbow and rib, balancing as carefully as one can in heels at a bingo parlor. The rest of the patrons filed out, and the owners began turning down lights.

"I'm sure you could get a bag if you asked," suggested a deep voice behind her.

Emma's cheeks flushed and she stumbled just enough to spill the armful of accoutrements across the table and onto the floor on the other side. "Geez," she breathed, "don't you watch where you're talking?"

Jake rested one hand on the back of her hip, just far enough from her ass to be polite, but low enough that she longed for more. Leaned over her to help pick up the daubers.

"I'd apologize," he whispered into her ear as she brought her head upright. "But seeing as there are multiple examples of you tripping over yourself this weekend, I don't think you need my help."

She let his breath melt against her flesh. *I'm only tripping over you,* she thought, but didn't say.

Emma steadied her center of balance, then got down on her knees to collect some daubers which had rolled under the table.

As her head moved down past his loins, Jake whispered, "damn, woman, you don't have to hit the gas so hard."

Now it was her turn to wield some sexual power. She paused with her head right at his crotch, and looked up at him through her eyelashes. Out of the corner of her eye she saw movement in his pants. She smiled at her power, and crawled further under the table, this time pushing her curvy ass up and out. She felt him step back and blow out all the air in his lungs, and she took her time collecting the fallen items.

Eventually, Jake knelt down beside her, first checking the hall to make sure it was empty, "you're amazing," he whispered. "That was really fun earlier."

The heat rose in her belly again, and all she could do was mutter hmm-hmm.

Emma remained in the prone position, and Jake ran a capped dauber across her back and around the curve of her backside. "I was wondering," he spoke with a crackling voice, "if you'd be interested in round two?"

She breathed in. "Hmm-mmm" was all she could get out. She knew if she tried to talk, she'd probably squeak.

Jake moved the bingo dauber around her skirt and onto the flesh of her thigh. She bit her lip as he trailed under her skirt and found her pussy, pushing against her folds with the capped tip of the dauber.

She blushed wickedly "are you about to fuck me with that thing?"

"I'm thinking about it." He bent got down on his knees and slid his face under hers, reaching for her lips with his mouth. She kissed him eagerly, and this time he slid the dauber deep inside her.

She let him penetrate it in and out of her a few times, then moaned sadly. "Now this isn't fair," she whined, and Jake raised an eyebrow at her. She kissed his mouth again and whined, "This dauber is no match for the much bigger things I've had in there just this evening."

She trailed a finger down his chest, across his stomach, and to the waist of his jeans, pulling at the button.

Jake groaned.

CHAPTER NINE

She shoved her hand into his pants and tugged at the length of him.

He grumbled, "You aren't playing fair either."

"Playing fair at what? Bingo? or sex?"

"Both," he croaked, and pulled the dauber out of her body, throwing it on the ground. He hoisted her up on his still-clothed hips and carried her back toward her office, clutching at her lips with his own.

"Why are we moving?" she whispered as she pulled her mouth away from his and clutched her legs tighter around his body, feeling his hardness against her heat. "I thought that was fun," motioning her head toward the bingo hall.

"Oh, it was," he grabbed at her neck with his teeth, "but I don't keep condoms in the public areas of this building."

She laughed. "Well, now you know you should."

He turned his body around and used his back to push open the office door, swinging her around to throw her onto the desk again.

She angled her body backward. "I'm glad you didn't have time to clean this up after last time."

"You mean an hour ago?" He teased. "Yeah, I was quick, but not that quick."

"Quick is good, when it's done right," she teased him back, and turned her body over to reach toward the drawer he'd pulled a condom out of before.

Jake grabbed at her ass and hoisted her skirt up, groaning a slow "Yes, that'll do."

She looked back up at him wickedly. "Don't get any ideas before your business is taken care of." She signaled her eyes down toward his erection, and fumbled her hand around in the drawer searching for protection.

He leaned over her backside, running his hand down her arm into the drawer and pressing his cock against her ass. She felt his tip brush her mound and moaned. Part of her just wanted it hard and naked and raw. Her rational side knew that would be trouble. She could sense he wanted the same thing as he furiously scrambled in the top drawer, too.

"Where are they," she half cried, propping her body over the edge of the desk and throwing other items out of the drawer.

Jake moaned, "I might be out." He pulled his cock away from her heat and she almost wept.

"How can you be out? We used one! How often do you have lovers in here?" She asked, but it was rhetorical. She didn't want to think about that right now. She just wanted him inside her.

"I'm sorry," he stepped back, releasing his grip on her hips.

Inside, she sobbed, and relaxed her frustrated body, turning over to edge off the desk and face him. "Shhh," she soothed, and kissed his hot lips. "We don't have to be done." She undid the rest of his pants and forced them to the floor, feeling his softer cock grow hard again.

"Don't tempt me into dangerous activity, woman," he snarled at her, but bit her lips back, growling.

She used his nuts as stress balls for a moment before grabbing at his huge dick and running her hands up and down it. Maybe she couldn't have it in her pussy, but she would definitely have it inside her one way or the other. "Come around the desk, boss."

He didn't have a clue what she was doing, but he rounded the desk like a puppy on steroids. She lay down on her back and hung her head off the edge, in front of the drawer that had let them down. She opened her lips.

He grunted, and offered the tip of his penis, which she lapped at eagerly before indicating that she could take more. He eased in carefully, groaning, and his position allowed him the opportunity to run a hand down her stomach and into her heat while she sucked at him. As he shoved two fingers into her hot pussy, she moaned and sucked more of him in. His knees began to buckle as he pushed into her mouth as far as she could let him. He dove into her mouth with his dick and her into pussy with his fingers, and she sucked and moaned at him, faster and harder, until her wetness soaked both the desk and his hand. She wanted his huge cock in there so badly, but this was a fair trade. He knew just where to hit the inside of her body with his fingers.

He opened a drawer with the other hand and she heard him pull something out, something plastic that rattled. He removed the hand from her body and traded whatever it was from the free hand to it, then she felt something cold and round enter inside her. She tried to release his dick from her mouth to ask what was happening, but he shushed her and jammed her body full, the cock in her mouth and the plastic balls in her pussy.

Plastic balls, she thought. Bingo balls. She was the cage now, and he was spinning her. She devoured him excitedly.

He left the balls in her pussy and moved his hand up her labia to her hot spot, rubbing one finger on each side of her clitoris. She shrieked and sucked him harder, moving one hand up to play with his balls, and the other to pull down her dress and expose her breast. She was getting close to orgasm, and she could tell he was, too. He moved faster, as deep as he could go in her throat, and he rubbed her clit harder. Her knees buckled and she moaned wildly as she climaxed, the bingo balls slowly popping back out of her body one at a time.

Jake chuckled at this as he too went weak. He pulled his cock to the tip of her lips and ejaculated cleanly, partly into her mouth but mostly down her bare neck and onto her nipple and the desk. She licked her lips and swallowed what salty fluid had landed in her mouth, humming a thank you for not gagging her completely. He too moaned a thank you and pulled his underwear back over his hips. She whined, already missing his fullness.

Jake reached for a towel behind the desk and offered it to her to clean up the spillage on her neck. She thanked him and began to sit up, wondering how many balls were still inside her.

He sensed her hesitation. "I think they all came out when you orgasmed," he said, looking at the array of moist bingo balls on the desk and floor.

"Well," she tried to look slightly more refined as she cleaned the cum off her neck. "I've never done that before."

"What? Bingo balls," Jake laughed. "Yeah, I've never done those either. Always wanted to see what would happen, though."

Emma playfully punched him in the arm. "Glad I could be your science experiment," she teased.

He offered an arm to help her down off the desk, and she stumbled slightly upon landing, her knees still weak from the sex. He caught her and held her close, looking down into her eyes. "That was fun," he said, and kissed her hard. She let him sweep her into his muscular grip and devour her mouth for a moment, before catching her balance and pushing him off.

His kiss was enjoyable, but she remembered that she had to go. "Lola is probably--" she started, pointing her thumb toward the door. Then she looked back at the wet mess they'd left behind. "Do you need help with--" she trailed off and his eyes followed her gaze.

"Oh," he stammered. "No, I got this. It's part of the job to make sure the hall is cleaned up." He laughed at himself a little, then grabbed a carton of kitchen wipes off a filing cabinet. "Go ahead. Uh, thank you again." He stumbled a little as he picked a yellow B-5 off the desk and wiped it down.

Cleanup would be awkward no matter what, she admitted to herself, and she stepped back toward the door. She spotted her underwear in the corner between the door and the wall, and she swooped down to grab at it. "Probably shouldn't leave these here, either," she joked.

He smiled. "Tomorrow's Bingo crew probably wouldn't appreciate it," he laughed, then added, "Thanks again."

She opened the office door and entered the darkened bingo hall, nearly skipping toward the exit doors. *Well, that was pretty wild,* she noted as she spotted Lola coming back up the fire escape stairs to the door. *But just in time.*

Lola pulled at the main door, but it was locked from the inside. Emma grabbed the daubers and bags and stepped up her speed. As she approached the door, she double-checked that she had all her belongings with her. She spotted the underwear still in her hand and freaked out, tucking it behind her back and opening the door for her friend.

Lola panted, "Sorry babe, were you waiting long?"

"I was about to ask you the same thing," Emma said.

Lola grabbed a few items off of Emma and didn't notice the underwear. Lola took the stairs first and Emma followed behind, holding the panties among her other items and wondering what to do with them. As they approached the parking lot, she spotted a dumpster. *It would be too weird to walk over and chuck them in there*, she thought.

Lola said, "Mabel had a ton of stuff to show me! Pictures of Hetty and some of her things. I totally lost track of time."

"It's okay," Emma insisted. "Jake gave me a tour of the office." *And his dick*, she smiled at herself.

They started toward downtown, their home still several blocks away by foot. Emma wondered how she was going to either dispose of the underwear or get it back on her body without Lola noticing.

Relief came when Lola stumbled in a pothole and dropped her bag, daubers rolling everywhere down James Street. As Emma grabbed Lola's bag to help pick everything up, she jammed her underwear in it as well.

"Thanks, my brain is going crazy," Lola remarked.

"Yours and mine both, babe" Emma stated. "Yours and mine both."

CHAPTER TEN

For the first Sunday in a long time, Emma woke up early with a clear head. A deep, dreamless sleep had left her smiling and refreshed, yet wondering what to do with all the extra time in the day. On a typical Sunday she'd nurse a hangover in bed for a few hours, sometimes in a stranger's bed, then groggily try to get home to slog through chores and laundry for the work week ahead. The previous night's mix of sober Bingo and hot sex had given her brain the rest it had craved so many other weekends.

She slipped quietly out of her room into the kitchen.

"You're up early," Lola was lying on the couch flipping through a decorating magazine. A carafe was steaming on the coffee table.

"So are you," Emma grabbed a mug and pattered over to the sofa, squeezing her bottom between Lola's feet and the cushions.

Lola made a small effort to shift out of her way, but Emma got the sense that her roommate was happy to use her butt as a foot warmer. "You know me, I'm always up early."

Emma poured herself a coffee from the carafe, and held her mug between her chilly hands. "Why is that? You and I keep the same hours, we drink the same drinks on most weekends, we work the same schedule, we often go home with different men every weekend, and yet you're always up. It's as though you never sleep."

"I sleep," Lola flipped another page then threw the magazine on the table. "Maybe I just do it differently."

"It must be a metabolism thing," Emma looked down at her soft rolls, then at her friend's lean physique, and frowned in envy.

"You don't do so bad," Lola smiled.

Emma eyed her curiously. "How much do you know?"

"Nothing, but I have a clue!" Lola reached her hand under her back and pulled out Emma's underwear. Emma blushed and grabbed at it, but Lola was too quick for her and held it just out of her reach. "Nuh-uh, lady. You don't get this back until you tell me everything. You weren't just 'learning how Bingo works,' were you?"

"Well, I definitely screamed Bingo a few times," Emma laughed.

Lola giggled but made no motion to hand the panties back. Emma faked a frown, but was eager to dish about Jake, so she told Lola everything.

#

An hour later, after much commentary and penis size comparison, the coffee was long gone and the two women were beside themselves in giggles. As Emma cleared the mugs and padded back to the kitchen, Lola followed her.

Lola said, "You like this guy."

"Well of course," Emma winked and held up the coffee carafe, hinting at his penis size.

Lola grinned again. "No, silly, you've never gushed about any of your pickups like this the next day."

"You said yourself, those guys are all boring corporate lawyers. This Bingo caller thing really paid off for me this time."

"He must do something else besides Bingo calling. Did you learn anything else about him?"

Emma rinsed the glasses in water and shook them out. "Well, he had some official paperwork from Microsoft on his desk, but I didn't read it. I was too busy pushing it off to make room for my butt." She wiggled her ass as she passed by, and Lola spanked her, laughing.

A cellphone twittered, and for a brief moment Emma's heart leapt hoping Jake had tracked her down and called. Then, inwardly she admonished herself for caring in the first place, and also because she hadn't shared numbers with him.

As Lola went to answer the call, Emma moved to her room to grab her phone, just in case. Then once again she felt inwardly embarrassed for wanting contact with Jake after their one-night, two-bang stand. She promised herself she'd forget about him, she would just have to get back into her normal rhythm. She grabbed a laundry basket and began circling her room, scooping up whatever clothing was on the floor.

When she came upon last night's dress, she rubbed it against her cheek instinctively, remembering what it was like to feel Jake slide it up her thighs and cum so carefully down her neck that he avoided hitting it. She almost wished he hadn't been so tidy, and that she'd have something dirty of his to lick later.

Again, she admonished herself and plunged the dress into the laundry basket, hiding it under some other items so that it wouldn't have this effect on her anymore.

As she entered the kitchen, she heard Lola's side of a distressed conversation.

"I'm so sorry." A pause. "There is nothing wrong with you." Lola looked to Emma with a pleading smile. "Of course you can. Emma and I can't wait to see you." Lola walked to the window, nodding and placating the person on the other end of the line. "Okay then, let me know."

Lola hung up the phone and stared at it, then looked around the living room.

Emma recognized the mental calculations of someone planning to turn their living space into a spare bedroom. "Was that Kiki?"

"Yes," Lola's shoulders slumped, but she stuck her tongue out of her mouth playfully. "Kier is on her way up from Portland to stay with us."

"Is Brent coming too?"

"Oh, Brent is 'coming' all right," Lola put her hands on her hips. "He's cumming right into his secretary."

Emma put the laundry basket down and ran to her friend, as though Lola was the one being cheated on. "What a bastard! How could he do this to her?"

Lola hugged her weakly then looked back at her phone. "Men!"

"Right? Those assholes!" It was Emma's turn to put her hands on her hips and stomp around. In doing so, she spotted her underwear on the floor and had another flashback to the night before. This time she wondered just how awesome Jake was at all. Was he married too? She hadn't noticed a ring, but truthfully she hadn't even been looking. It was a one-night stand. *It was just a one-night stand. I have to stop thinking about him.* She scooped the panties off the floor and tucked them deep into the bottom of the laundry basket as well. The memories would fade after a good soak in the laundry machine, she was certain.

She was wrong, though. Her attention lingered on the dirty clothes and she'd missed the fact that Lola was still talking. "So we'll have to set this space up today."

"What? Huh?" Emma turned her body away from the laundry basket and mentally kicked herself for pining again.

"She's coming now. I don't know how long she'll stay."

"Now? Doesn't she have a job? What about Tor?" Emma spitfired the questions then quickly caught herself again and reconsidered her condemnation. "I mean, she's welcome for as long as she needs, of course. Sorry, I'm just a bit flustered." *In more ways than one.*

Lola frowned. "Tor is in college, remember? I bet not having him home is part of the reason Brent strayed. In any case, Ki is between jobs. I think she just needs to sit down and sort out what she's going to do."

"Of course," Emma stated. "I'll go do laundry while you get started making this room into a bedroom. Let me do your clothes as well so you don't have to think about it."

Lola's face softened into relief, and she ran to her room to get her already bagged laundry.

As Emma fished around for change in their coin jar and opened the door, she said, "I hope you realize this bag of clothes won't be as neatly sorted when it comes back to you."

Lola laughed, but looked a little apprehensive, too. "If you think I'm too neat, wait 'til you really get to know Kier. Oh, and if you call her Kiki to her face, she's going to throttle you."

"Wow," Emma rolled her eyes as she opened the door to the hallway. "You're so lucky you have a big sister."

CHAPTER ELEVEN

he rhythmic hum of laundry had certainly eased her mind. Emma thought about the last time she'd seen Kiki—*Kier,* she reminded herself. It had possibly been years now. She couldn't believe Kier's son Tor was in college now, and that her husband was cheating on her. Both Lola and Emma had looked up to Kier so much when they were younger. The age difference between them and Kier was big, it was easy to watch her life from the outside and long for it. Brent was so handsome and so wonderful to her, Lola had always said. Emma felt anger on behalf of her best friend and roommate. Never mind that Kier was suffering a cheating husband, Lola, who'd been raised without a father, must be looking at men a different way now, too.

As the machine hummed, Emma glared at her phone in wanton anticipation, but realized her need was unrequited. How could Jake find her when all he knew was her first name? She rolled her eyes at herself for her ridiculous attraction for the man. What made him different than the usual slough of lawyers she went through on any given weekend? Nothing. Nothing except that he obviously had an impact on kids and the elderly alike. Nothing except that his hard body melted at her touch. Nothing, except that he was smoking hot and rode her so hard she got wet just thinking about him. Her body began to ache at the memory.

Alone in the basement laundry room she felt warm and excited again. *I must definitely be ovulating,* she considered as she felt the heat rise in her belly, *that's the only reason this man would affect me so much.*

In considering her current biological state, she wondered about the possibilities available to heal herself. She could find a bathroom and privately rub one out with a couple of fingers, which would only take a minute or two, or she could go back upstairs and lock herself in her room with a dildo. That would be a few more minutes and may draw the attention of her roommate. She could also leave the building altogether and find an easy pickup at the bar across the road. *It* is *tourist season,* she thought to herself.

But her body lost mojo at that thought, and her brain fixated on Jake instead. A tourist wouldn't do when compared to the wild adventure she'd had last night. *Bingo balls in my hotbox--who can top that the next day?*

Emma approached the laundry machine as it purred in the corner. She touched it with her fingers, feeling it's soft shake and wondering if all those old stories of ladies on their laundry machines was a real thing, or just some strange male fantasy.

She pushed her belly against the machine and it rattled her inside, but hardly seemed sexy. She tilted her hips so that her clitoris touched the metal through her sweatpants, and although it was hot, it was barely orgasm-worthy.

She looked back over her shoulder to make sure she was the only tenant in the room, then hopped up on the machine, spreading her legs and letting her body feel the machine through her pajamas. It hummed and shook lightly under her, but barely had an effect. *Well, so much for that lie. Thanks for nothing, Hollywood.*

Footsteps sounded in the hallway, and Emma scurried to right herself and get off the machine as quickly as possible.

Lola's voice preceded her around the corner. "We should probably wash these dish towels, and--what the hell are you doing?" She stumbled slightly upon seeing Emma leap down from the laundry machine.

"Nothing, I was uh..."

Lola's left eyebrow raised inquisitively, but a smirk formed across her lips.

Emma wobbled on her feet. "Would you believe I was looking behind the machine for quarters?" She gawked pleadingly at her roommate, then both girls erupted into laughter.

"No, no I wouldn't. So," Lola laughed and eyed the laundry machine up and down. "How was it for you?"

"Not that fun, actually. I'm pretty sure we've been lied to all these years."

The machine rumbled, and Lola opened it quickly to throw the towels in. "Were you doing it right?"

"There's a wrong way?" Now it was Emma's turn to give the machine the once over with her eyes.

"I don't know! Don't look at me, I'm not the one humping an appliance!" Lola pushed on the machine, and Emma sensed she wanted to try it out, too.

"Go on then," Emma prodded, "Don't let me be the only horny bastard in the room."

"I have a feeling our sex lives are going to take a nose-dive once Kier gets here. She's kind of square." Lola hoisted her body up on the machine and shifted her legs around, feeling the rumble of the machine.

Emma laughed at her. "Well?"

"You're right, there's not much there. Quick, turn the dial to spin and let's see if that does it!"

Emma leaned around Lola and stretched her arm toward the dial, her breasts brushing against Lola's knees. She remarked on the ridiculousness of the situation. "I can't believe I'm trying to help my best friend achieve orgasm on a laundry machine."

"Well," Lola teased, "You could squeeze up here and we could try it together." She shifted her body to the right.

Emma squeezed up between the coin slot and Lola's thigh, giggling. "Don't you ever tell anyone about our three-way with the Kenmore."

"We'll call him Ken," Lola said as the spin cycle began.

The machine rattled and hummed, and the women shifted awkwardly into multiple bizarre positions to find the hottest spots. Ultimately, the effect was minimal, but the laughing that transpired was enough of an endorphin rush for both of them.

As the spin cycle came to an end, they teetered off the machine, giggling madly. "So that's that," Lola said. "If anyone ever asks us if a three-way is worth it, we can honestly tell them no."

"I'm pretty sure the machine liked it!" Emma looked at the laundry machine, which seemed to purr much louder than before. She patted it like a boy toy, and both women erupted into laughter again.

CHAPTER TWELVE

After the wash cycle, the two women loaded the clothes into the dryer and went back upstairs. Emma promised to come down in an hour when the dry cycle was done, and not have sex with the dryer without her best friend there, too. "This threesome thing is just for appliances, right? I don't have to share lovers with you, do I?"

"You should, you're getting more than me. I'm a little bit jealous of your tryst last night and I'm wondering if there is any action at Bingo for me."

"There were a couple of handsome older gentlemen," Emma mused, "if you like oxygen tanks and 1960s cologne."

"I bet they have some experience," Lola said thoughtfully, then winked.

As they opened the door to the apartment, Emma noted that many of Hetty's knickknacks weren't in their usual spots. "Wow, you move fast." She moved to the shelf where her favorite little items usually lay. "Where are the cats playing piano?"

"They're in a box in your room, for now." Lola moved to the bookshelf and began pulling out a few of the dustier old remnants. "It's for personal sanity, I'm sorry. My sister will ridicule me if she sees how many of these old things I insist on keeping."

"It's no problem at all, babe. I'll take care of all of it while she's here, but what's her deal?"

"She just thinks I'm unable to move on from Grandma's death, and I'm tired of arguing with her about it."

"Hey, no excuses needed. You and Hetty were close. Hell, I was close with her, too. I would want to keep her stuff. Does your sister not have keepsakes?"

"No, she didn't have the same connection to Grandma as I had. It's just as well we get through this visit without her nagging me to move on." Lola began to talk inwardly to herself. "I *have* moved on."

Emma put an arm on Lola's shoulder. "I know you have, babe. Your sister will see it, too."

"Will she? I don't think so." Lola moved to the window, turned around and looked back into the small apartment. "Look at us, Emma. We're in our mid-thirties and we still live together like we're a college sorority, and I'm hanging on to ridiculous old people stuff." She grabbed a teacup and saucer off a doily on the windowsill and shook it.

Emma looked around the room, too. The furnishings were indeed of a style that didn't indicate young, hip Seattleites, but she liked that. It was cozy and made her feel like she was always welcome home somewhere. She smiled and took the dishes from Lola, walking back toward her room. "It's okay to like a certain style, Lola. It doesn't make you old, or attached, or unable to move on. It makes you a human with specific taste in décor."

"I know." Lola removed a doily from the windowsill. "Maybe my clock is ticking and I'm feeling it."

Emma returned from her room and scanned for more remnants of Hetty to remove. "The clock is a lie," she stated decidedly. "You're young. We're still young. We don't need to get married or have babies." Just then, her thoughts wandered to Jake, and she felt an unexplained emptiness in the depths of her belly. She stumbled and put a hand on her pelvis.

Lola noted this movement. "Everything okay?"

"I think so," Emma shook herself. "I just suddenly had a feeling I never wanted to have."

"Baby? Baby." Lola repeated the word slowly and watched Emma's reaction.

Emma's face fell and her shoulders weakened. "I'm not a baby person. I'm not."

"Oh my god, you are! You're thinking about babies right now!"

"Dear god," Emma shivered and sat down on the sofa. "What the hell is wrong with me?"

"You're ovulating. It happens. Maybe you're suddenly growing up. Let's go out tonight and get some lawyers. You can test them for diseases and then go condom free!" Lola threw herself down on the sofa beside Emma, laughing.

Emma scowled. "No. No lawyers. I'm done with that lifestyle."

"Are you actually considering finding a man and settling down," Lola inquired. "Not Jake, is it?"

"No, not Jake. That was nothing more than a booty call," Emma lied. She didn't bother telling her friend that it was the best booty call she'd ever had--twice!--and that he'd ruined her for one night stands forever.

Lola gave her a look as though she saw right through her, but Emma ignored it and mindlessly shuffled some couch cushions around.

CHAPTER THIRTEEN

Lola left the apartment to go pick up some fresh foods for Kier, who was far pickier an eater than the women.

Downstairs, the dryer had just finished, and the clothes were still toasty. Emma began folding a few as she pulled them out, but ultimately decided to just haul the gear out and sort it upstairs. The last thing she pulled out was the dress and panties from the night before, and she felt their soft cotton against her cheek before heaping them onto the basket and heading upstairs.

In the lobby of the building, she saw a dark shadow lurking through the beveled glass front door. She could make out a hat and muscular frame. The figure held a hand up to knock, then paused, and put the arm back down.

Emma looked down at her PJs and basket of laundry, wondering if she should help the poor soul out in her current state. *This is Seattle,* she said to herself, *people dress like me to go out all the time.* She ran to the door as the figure moved out of her line of sight, and pushed it open with her butt. A rush of damp

November air blew in and surprised her, being such a radical change from the t-shirt weather the night before. Through her thin pajamas every inch of her body felt kissed with electric cold. *Typical indecisive Seattle climate,* she thought as she righted herself and called out, "Hey, are you looking for someone?"

The figure turned, and Emma instantly recognized Jake's strong jaw. She gasped and another gust of cold wind blew her hair into her mouth. She sputtered.

"Hey," Jake appeared taken aback at her, then his eyes shot down to her chest. Emma looked down at herself. She was completely disheveled with her hair in her face, and the cold air had brought her nipples to standing attention. *Or was that him,* she wondered. She brought the laundry basket up from her hip and tried to shield herself from his gaze, although it was clearly too late. She was not the sexy vixen she'd been the night before, not by a long shot.

"Hey," she said back, and spotted his blush. Or was that just the cold wind, too? "Wait a minute, how did you find me?"

"I, uh," Jake stumbled from one foot to the next, stared down at the ground, and adjusted his hat. "I looked you up."

"How? How did you look me up?" The wind blew again, and this time she realized her nipples were responding. She nodded her head back into the apartment, indicating that Jake should come too. No sense having a conversation in the cold.

Jake moved to the door and held it while she went back inside toward the staircase, then he followed her. "This is super creepy, I realize that." He looked back as the door closed behind him.

"And that's why you tried to leave just now?" she followed his gaze out the door.

He nodded. "I had a lot of fun last night," he offered, and seemed to be on the verge of saying something else, but let it drop.

"I did too," she smiled at him, and his shoulders seemed to ease. "Come upstairs and you can explain yourself." She led the way to the small apartment, extremely grateful to the universe that it had been madly cleaned just twenty minutes ago.

She put the laundry basket down on the sofa, and Jake's eyes naturally fell to it and darkened lasciviously. "I recognize those clothes," he nodded toward the dress and panties. "I hope you weren't eager to wash me off."

Emma laughed. "They're Lola's. I borrowed them. This is Lola's apartment. Everything is Lola's." *Stop talking, stop talking!* "Except my room, which is over there." *Really brain, please stop talking.* Jake's eyes widened at the misinterpreted invitation, and Emma quickly righted herself and switched on her left brain. "You haven't told me what you're doing here or how you found me."

Immediately he blushed again. "Yeah, that. I looked up your full name by going through last night's credit card statements."

"Woah, that's--"

"Weird, I know! That's why I turned away outside." He unconsciously backed toward the apartment door.

"I could have come to see you next weekend." Emma attempted to look busy focusing on the clothes. As she folded the dress, her body lit on fire with the memory of their crazy sex the previous night. She swore she felt her womb cry out in want.

"That's the thing. This was my last week. I'm leaving."

"You're leaving Bingo?"

"I'm leaving Seattle. I'm moving to Portland--today, actually." Jake waved his hand out the window. "My car is loaded up."

Emma looked toward the window, frantic for something to say to keep him around longer. *It was just a one-night stand,* her brain reminded her. *Shut up, brain!* cried her uterus. "What about the soccer kids? Aidan?"

"I had to quit coaching. The Bingo was only temporary. I'm actually a Corporate--"

"Don't say it!" Emma's horror bled into her face, causing Jake to stare puzzled at her. If this was another one-nighter with a lawyer, it was a sure sign that Emma was destined to a future of them.

Jake finished slowly, in the form of a question "-- Development Manager?"

"Oh, whew." Emma put a hand on her chest and slumped her body in relief. Jake watched her with a curious stare. Emma realized how confused he must be and attempted to change the subject back to where it was. "So, you're in Biz Dev, got it. Biz devs are some of my favorite people. Why Portland?"

Jake made a motion to remove his jacket, then paused as though looking for confirmation that his behavior was welcome and not creepy. Emma smiled and nodded toward the back of the sofa. He tossed it and moved further into the small living room, making himself more comfortable. She noted how his frame devoured the living space, and how it still seemed like a grandma's apartment with such a modern hot body in it. Jake continued talking as he neared the window. "I don't know if you're aware of the latest round of layoffs at Microsoft, but..."

"Of course I'm aware of them," Emma interjected, "I'm working on a lot of them!" At this, Jake's eyebrow shot up, and Emma balked. "I work in HR."

"Ah," Jake chuckled. "So, I can thank you for the loss of my job? I should have known you were a devil woman."

"That's not fair!" Emma tossed a clean shirt at him and laughed. He caught it and mindlessly began folding it for her. She said, "I'm not in charge of flattening orgs or budgeting, I just do the paperwork."

"Ah, you might have seen my name on the pile, then." He stood from the chair and brought the neatly folded shirt to the pile she'd started.

Her body tingled as he moved beside her and grabbed the next tee shirt, his body just touching hers enough to tickle the hairs on her arm, but not so close as to be awkward about doing such a personal chore.

"I may have, it was a long list." She quickly stashed some panties on her side of the basket, a move he noted but tried his best not to respond to. "Also, I don't actually know your full name."

"Hi, nice to meet you Emma Soledad," he held a folded tee in his arms and bent his other arm out to her, then whispered through a grin "Please try to forget that I only know your full name because I looked up your credit card information."

She chuckled and grasped his hand. Shivers ran through her body.

His voice returned to its normal sultry tone, "my name is Jake Ono."

Flustered, she ran the name around her mouth. "Jake Ono. Wait, Jacob Ono?" She withdrew her hand and paced across the room to the desk, rifling through papers. "I think I did process your paperwork." When she found what she was looking for, she held it up. "Partner business development manager for Xbox Devices, huh?" Then she looked at him again. She analyzed his face for some kind of recognition, then apologized for staring. "I thought he'd be Japanese."

He furrowed his brow, and without thinking about it grabbed another garment to fold out of the basket. It turned out to be a sexy pair of underwear, which he gawked at for a brief moment before stashing it in the basket again. "Wow," he said.

Emma laughed. "Don't get any ideas, those are Lola's."

He shrugged. "I'll have you know I'm a quarter Japanese, so you're not that far off."

Jake noted her contemplation. "It's mostly in the hair." He ran a hand through his shiny dark locks and blew a stray hair out of the way. "Wait 'til you meet my brother, though. He is unmistakably Japanese."

Emma swallowed hard, processing what he'd just said. Jake caught himself and seemed to stumble over it, too.

A one-night stand intends for me to meet his brother? She tried to think of something to say, but nothing came out.

As though he were doing the same thing, he made a movement to speak, but second-guessed himself and moved back to the laundry, this time making sure he grabbed a more appropriate garment to fold.

Emma put the paper back on the desk and slowly returned to the laundry bin, grabbing a few dish towels and soundlessly taking them to the kitchen to hang on the oven door.

When Jake had run out of tees and other, more practical items, he stared awkwardly into the basket at a pile of underwear and one bra. "I shouldn't have stalked you, I'm sorry." He looked like a lost child who didn't know where to go.

Emma tried to soften the weirdness. "It's okay, really. I'm glad you let me know you're moving to Portland, actually. I would have gone to Bingo next weekend, and probably the weekend after that, and wondered whether the sex was so bad you'd run away."

"That big of a fan of Bingo, are you?" Jake's tension seemed to fall away smoothly, and his color returned. His pecs pushed through his thin knit shirt.

Emma caught herself staring. "I'm beginning to warm up to the game." Trying to end the pain of a screaming sexless womb, she frantically grabbed at the remaining underwear in the basket and turned toward Lola's room.

Jake followed her, and with each step she took toward Lola's dresser, his presence seemed to make itself ever clearer to her wanting body. She dove for the dresser and threw the underwear into the first drawer she could reach, then spun around to take in another look at Jake's delicious body. She could not resist herself if she tried, and she knew it. Jake seemed to wait, as though not wanting to come on too strong, but one look toward his pants and she knew he was dying inside, too, afraid to make the wrong move.

He's moving to Portland, her brain reminded herself. *Today!*

He's the best we've ever had, her womb seemed to scream at her. So, she leapt at him.

He wrapped his arms around her, lifted her off the ground to his full height, and planted his lips firmly against hers. She sought out his lips with her teeth and nibbled at him, and he threw her to the bed.

Searching for condoms, her hands moved frantically toward a nightstand that wasn't there. "It's okay," Jake said and whipped off her pajama bottoms, "I have one." His pants came off within seconds.

"Wait," she tried to whisper, but her body was sending too many signals otherwise, and he was reading them like an adolescent reads Hustler.

"Hmm-mm" he grunted into her neck, as he slid the condom on with one hand and pushed the rest of his pants to the floor.

"This isn't--" her body screamed at her to shut up, her nipples hardening and her pussy growing so wet she was going to cum on his mere pheromones alone. "This isn't my... room."

The last word was hushed into nothingness as Jake thrust his huge cock into her body. Soon, she'd forgotten what she was even saying, and let her brain shut completely down, allowing her nerve endings to take over full control of her senses.

Jake grunted some sort of agreement with what she was saying, but neither of them were thinking anymore. As he pulled his dick back out of her pussy, she whined in want and scratched at his shoulders. He pushed her shirt up over her breasts, swallowing them with his eyes for a brief moment before wrapping his arm around the back of her neck and throwing all of himself back inside her even deeper. She moaned in agony, and he kissed her down her neck as he thrust himself into her body again. Emma grabbed at his head and ran her fingers through his smooth hair. Jake moved his head down to her breasts and tickled her right nipple with his tongue, an action that sent a bolt of lightning down through her womb. She screeched and squeezed him tighter, which made him moan and thrust harder.

Emma clutched for the bedsheets as her body reached toward orgasmic ecstasy, and found they weren't where they usually were. She remembered again that she was in Lola's room, and worried about the mess her wet orgasm would make. "Jake..." she pleaded.

He took this as a sign to finish, wrapped one arm under her leg in order to get deeper, and pumped her harder and faster. Again, she forgot where she was, and moved deeper into the clutches of his other, strong arm, wailing in desire.

A female voice said, "This is quite a welcome."

"Well, hello." Lola's voice interjected between moans. Jake released Emma's body at lightning speed and he dropped her to the sheets, clutching at whatever he could find to cover himself up. Emma whelped miserably, her body instantly empty at the departure, and her brain not fully recognizing the embarrassing situation they'd been found in.

She pulled her thoughts together, and straightened her t-shirt over her boobs and lady bits as well as she could, given that her swollen breasts and erect nipples seemed to make her upper body even bigger. In the end, bolting upright into a sitting position seemed to offer the least view.

For a moment, Kier and Lola merely stared at them, their eyebrows raised with questions. Although a good thirteen years separated them in age, they could not be confused for anything but sisters.

Emma's face flushed and she scrambled to give Jake more privacy, blocking him with her body. He'd already been quick enough to pull his pants back up, but his still-hard dick was clearly too much for any zippers or buttons. Emma tried to speak, but nothing came to mind.

Kier's mouth was open still in shock, an extra set of mid-forties eyebrow wrinkles deepening in concern, but Lola tilted her head a bit to get a better look at Emma's catch, and her mouth expanded into a wicked smile. "Laundry was a success, then?"

"Lola, I--" Emma scrambled to pull her pajamas back up her legs as quick as possible, but her body was weakened from sex and she tripped and put both legs down one pantleg. She fell backwards onto the bed and madly attempted to correct herself.

Jake, silently trying to dress himself on the floor, was now seemingly recovered and began to stand up, his shoulders looming large over the three women, lined with muscles still taut from his own pleasure. A bead of sweat rolled down his neck. All three ladies unconsciously licked their lips.

"Lo, I'll just be in the kitchen putting your groceries away." Kier still looked half confused, half disgusted, but her eyes lingered on Jake an extra few seconds before she retreated.

Jake smiled shyly and scratched the back of his neck.

Lola moved into the room and closed the door, a wicked grin still plastered across her face. She reached out a hand for a shake, purposefully holding it too low, flirting with his still unbuttoned pants. Emma watched his eyes scan Lola's amazing body once, and his pants tented ever so slightly. Rather than feel envy, her body just wanted to finish what they'd started even more.

Jake shuffled from one foot to another, as though adjusting himself as best as possible, and he reached to shake the hand in front of him. "Lola, right?" He took the other arm down from behind his neck and placed his hand on Emma's shoulder, as though steadying her. "Hi, I'm Jake."

"Yes," Lola teased, "I believe we met at Bingo." She shook his hand firmly then moved her hands to her hips in condemnation.

Emma found her bearings and stood, not knowing whether to brush Jake's arm off her shoulder or leave it there. In the end, he shifted both hands to his pants anyway, ready now to zip them up.

"Lola, I can explain," she said. A million things ran through her head, but none of them were decent excuses. "Actually, I really can't explain."

Lola scowled at her, then lightened. "You have a room of your own, you know." She bent slightly to peer around Emma at her waylaid sheets. "Then again, my bed hasn't had much action lately. I'm sure it appreciates it."

Jake was still awkwardly watching the two women, his body language indicating he didn't know whether to stay or run.

Emma felt instant embarrassment on his behalf. He probably didn't realize that walking in on sex was something quite common in their small apartment. She tried to laugh, to help him understand that it was really no big deal. "Jake was just here to--" *just what? What had he come over to do?* She realized he'd never had an opportunity to say anything to her besides the fact that he was moving to Portland.

Jake's voice squeaked a bit as he spoke, Emma wondered if it was remnants of the unfortunate sexual letdown. "I was actually here to invite Emma to dinner tonight so we could, uh, chat." His eyes darted back to the bed and he blushed, clearly humiliated that he'd skipped a real date and leapt right into bed. The wrong bed.

"Yes, a date. He was just here for dinner," Emma chimed, happy to have a real excuse for her man candy to be in the apartment.

Lola's eyebrow remained taught, but it was done sarcastically rather than critically. "Sure, dinner. I hope my girl was tasty." She opened the door and ushered them out. Jake went first, like a lightning bolt.

As Emma moved past her bestie, she whispered, "I'll wash the sheets."

"Yeah you will," Lola teased, and lightly punched her in the arm.

In the living room, Kier was pretending to peruse the decor magazine, but her eyes were glued on Jake, as though analyzing his perfect body for hints of photoshop. Emma was proud, but still embarrassed. "Hi Kier, I'm so glad you could make it."

"Emma, good to see you again." Kier turned to Lola and stated, "I hope that's not my room."

"Actually," Lola looked a little sick, "I thought you'd take the couch."

At this, Kier appeared thoroughly confused. "The couch? This is my apartment, too!" Then, catching Emma in the corner of her eye, she relented. "But I guess I didn't give much warning of my arrival."

Jake began pulling his boots on as fast as possible. Emma grabbed his coat and her own and went to open the apartment door. As Jake bolted clean out of the space, she paused at the door. "It's okay, Kier can have my room." Looking from Lola's frustrated face to Kier's horrific glare, she added, "it's clean. I'll catch up with you two later tonight."

As she closed the apartment door behind her and trailed after Jake, she heard the sisters begin to bicker. *Just like old times.* She didn't wait to listen about what.

CHAPTER FOURTEEN

Jake was already out on the sidewalk, shuffling from one foot to the other, as though eager to run as far away as possible. The cold air bit at Emma's cheeks, and as she approached him, she fumbled with the zipper on her coat. Jake absentmindedly slipped an arm around her waist and pulled her into him. "That was probably the most embarrassing moment of my year," he said toward the street, his pink cheeks made more so by the biting cold.

"It's fine, really," Emma assured him. "Lola and I have a lot of ridiculous accidents like that, although I haven't accidentally done it in her bedroom in a while. Just earlier today she and I had a three-way with Ken."

"Wait wait wait, who?" Jake moved his hands to her shoulders and searched her face as though looking for her Pinocchio nose to grow.

She winked at him mischievously, waved a hand at him, and turned to lead him toward some of the restaurants in Pioneer Square. "I'll tell you about it when we run out of dinner topics, I promise. What I'm saying is that you shouldn't be embarrassed about Lola. Kier? sure, but she's a temporary guest. Accidents happen."

"You're very levelheaded about all of this." Jake skipped after her and held her arm as they walked down Yesler to 1st street. She smiled at his concern, it sure beat screwing a lawyer and being left a note the next day.

"I'm in HR, we try not to show too much empathy."

"I felt that at my layoff," Jake said, trying to feign anger but tilting the corner of his mouth in a wry smile.

They walked north, passing a few pizza joints and finally settling on a seafood and oyster bar. For a Sunday night in a big tourist area, the place was not very crowded. As they waited for their table, Emma wondered how best to broach her subject without upsetting him about the layoffs. In the end, being completely direct seemed to be their thing, so why not just flat-out ask?

"So," she said. "Speaking of layoff, what's in Portland?"

Jake seemed excited. "I tried to interview locally but nothing really hooked me, you know? I'm not dying for cash, so I feel like I have the opportunity to do things that matter."

The host beckoned them to follow her to a table, and Emma nodded at him to keep talking. They sat at a small table beside the window.

"So then an old friend tells me he's launching this little startup in Portland--and I'm talking startup, it's in some guy's garage--"

Emma laughed, "Of course, it's Portland. I have a feeling a lot of small businesses are in somebody's garage."

Jake chuckled. "Anyway, their product is awesome, but without venture capital they can't get off the ground enough to even pay their contractors to build the thing. So, since business development is my skillset, and since I still have a number of months to not worry about money, I figured I'd help them out."

"Do you have a place to stay?"

"For now, I'm just crashing on Mike's couch."

"This is very *The Social Network*." Emma called a server over for drinks. "Wine?"

Jake nodded. "The Facebook movie? I guess, yeah."

"Except those guys were college kids. You and your 'old' friend are--what?" She pondered his face for some sign of age. His skin barely showed a wrinkle. "Thirty-three?"

"Thirty-eight, thank you. But I see what you're saying." Jake shook his head and laughed at himself. "It's all very sudden, I know, I just felt like I needed a change. I've been working eleven-hour days at Microsoft for the past twenty years. I had a bit of a life on the side with the soccer volunteering and stuff, but time is getting away from me."

She knew what that felt like. "Tell me about the soccer." She sat back while the waiter poured a sample of the wine into her glass and waited for her to approve it. She never knew exactly what to do after that, so she sniffed at it a little and sipped, then nodded. To Jake she asked, "Do you have kids?"

"No. I got into soccer because I was having a fling with one of the soccer Moms." Jake blushed upon saying this, then straightened himself. "That relationship didn't last very long, but the kids were awesome, so I stayed on. I also ran the bingo games on the weekends because that's when my girlfriend--well, the Mom? What do you call the woman you're having commitment-free sex with?" Jake mused this for a moment. Emma's eyes widened and she gawked at him. He continued, "Anyway, she was with the family on weekends, so I had nothing else to do but volunteer for the soccer organization. In the end the relationship ended--"

"Did the Dad find out?"

"No, he was her soon-to-be Ex anyway. I just felt like an asshole and wanted more out of a relationship. Anyway, the fling ended and there I was, working long days, volunteering for this soccer club whenever I could, and running Bingo on weekends. It was busy, but I loved every second of it. I didn't even know I was missing anything. Then last Friday, there you were."

Emma flustered and shifted in her seat. "Me? I'm flattered but I could be anyone."

"Well, my usual clientele at the Bingo parlor are either eighty years old or much-too-young college kids. It's slightly possible I could have fallen for any--what? Thirty-two-year-old?"

"Thirty-five."

"--thirty-five-year-old that walked through my door, but there was something about the way you treated Aidan that made me second-guess every decision I've made in the last week. So here I am, just wanting to get to know the woman who rattled my ball cage one last time before I left for the City of Roses."

Emma blushed, flattered to the point where she had no words. Had he said he was falling for her? What does one say to that?

The server saved her by approaching for their order. Emma realized they hadn't even looked at a menu, but, desperate to prolong the ability to not look Jake in the eye, she picked up her menu and ordered the first pasta dish she saw.

Jake took a bit more time to peruse the menu but settled on an Alaskan salmon with King Crab.

Emma suddenly realized how hungry she was after a day of chores, unfinished sex, and no food, so when Jake was finished ordering she jumped in again. "Can I change my order? I'll take the steak and lobster dinner with an extra order of soup."

Jake's eyebrow raised.

Emma's cheeks reddened, both at the server's feigned interest and the ball cage rattling comment. She tried to think of something, anything, to change the subject. "So, besides the soccer mom, do you have any other relationships going on?"

Now it was Jake's turn to blush. "Do you actually want to talk numbers? Isn't that like third date material?"

Emma laughed and pondered that for a moment. "Isn't this kind of like a third date? We met on Friday over sodas,"

"Yeah, and you bailed on me pretty quick," Jake interjected.

"I spilled them all over myself. I went to go get cleaned up! It's not my fault you had to get back to work."

"It's a timed game with people who need to return to the old age home, of course I had to get back to work!" Jake and Emma laughed together for a moment, the awkwardness dissipating.

"Anyway," she continued, "Our second date was yesterday--"

At this, Jake winked. "And what a second date it was! If I'd known that I could get laid--"

"Twice, even!" Emma interjected, smiling.

"--after only the second date, I wouldn't have tried so hard with that soccer mom."

The food arrived and as they ate hungrily, the topic changed to slightly lighter things, like thoughts about the new CEO at Microsoft, transportation to and from Microsoft, and life at Microsoft.

"All we're talking about is Microsoft," Emma finally said. "I wonder if we have anything else in common."

Jake pondered that for a minute and then raised his hand. "Of course we have something else in common! We both really like sex!"

An older couple at the next table gawked at them but returned to their meals right away. *They're probably sex fiends too,* Emma thought, *I hope the fun doesn't stop with old age.* At this final thought, Emma's mind went to sex with Jake and she wondered if she'd ever have that kind of fun again. Random corporate lawyers were just not going to cut it after this. She would miss Jake's hard body, definitive musculature, huge cock and, she admitted to herself, him. Emma dove into her steak with vigor, laughing at his sex joke but not really knowing what else to say.

Jake seemed embarrassed enough by the disproportionately loud sex talk, and stuffed extra coleslaw into his mouth.

The two enjoyed the silence for a while, watching people of all shapes and sizes walk by on the street. A light rain had started and a few umbrellas popped open, clearly tourists as Seattleites didn't use umbrellas, and the rest of the passersby just raised their collars a bit and trudged on.

Finally, Jake spoke "I'll miss it. Seattle."

"I was just thinking about that. Did you pick out the tourists?"

"Anyone with an umbrella," Jake laughed.

CHAPTER FIFTEEN

Conversation over dinner stayed at the surface level, as the two got to know each other a little bit. They'd both gotten jobs at Microsoft via college internships, so they'd never done much outside of that. Jake talked about the potential in Portland with excited trepidation, as though he were a new explorer setting sail on the high seas. Emma watched his eyes alight with the potential the most hipster city in America offered him. Yes, he had binge-watched every episode of *Portlandia*.

When the bill arrived, Emma reached for it but Jake whisked it out of her hands.

"Now wait a minute," she protested, "I'm the employed one here and I ate the most."

"I'm a traditional guy," Jake insisted, throwing a gold card on the bill.

"Oh? Then this is not going to work at all. I'm my own person and can pay for myself." Emma took her own gold card out and threw it on top of Jake's, then she stared him down.

He didn't blink, but his lips curled in his quirky smile again. "*What's* not going to work?"

"I, uh," Emma blinked first, and Jake leaned back with a proud grin.

As the server walked by their table, he grabbed Emma's card and practically threw it at her. He handed the server his card instead. "I win."

Emma sputtered, but she was enjoying the back and forth. "It's your savings to blow through," she shrugged and stuffed her card back in her pocket with indignation. "I'm the only employed person at this table right now. In fact, I'm the only person with a guaranteed place to sleep tonight."

At this, Jake laughed. "Now that's a lie and you know it, we're both sleeping on couches tonight."

"Oh," Emma remembered their houseguest and how she'd offered up her bedroom on the way out the door. "Right."

The night air was colder now, and Jake held out his arm for her as they stepped out onto the sidewalk. She snuggled into him as a large gust of wind sent leaves careening up 1st street. She didn't want this evening to end, and yet she did. The sooner he was gone, the sooner she could start trying to forget about him. She wondered if he felt the same way.

After they crossed Columbia street, she finally asked, "Why'd you come here?"

"I told you." He said quickly, "I wanted to treat you to a proper dinner before I left."

"Yes, but why?"

"Because I'm not a typical one-night stand person. I don't like to do that," he said. "Do you do that?"

"Yes! I do it all the time!" There was no sense lying to him, she figured. "We never actually finished that numbers conversation, you know. Now I'm wondering just how many more lovers I've had than you. I feel like a slut."

"Well, it's settled then." He said, "I really like sluts." As they approached her apartment, he pulled her in close and kissed her.

She stopped walking and reveled in him devouring her lips, then her legs began to grow weak. "Careful now." She finally pulled away from his mouth. "You might bring out the slut again and we're both couch surfing right now, remember?"

He kissed her again briefly but withdrew with a groan. "We never got to finish that last time, either."

At the memory, her stomach fluttered and her body felt empty again. She really needed to finish that O. There would be no masturbating on the couch later either, she knew. That'd be too risky with two other people in their small apartment. She didn't want this one to end this way, she needed to feel him inside her again. Frantically, she looked around them. "Where's your car?"

"It's in the parking garage," Jake pointed to the large paid parking site up the road, the one Seattleites called the Sinking Ship for it's bizarre boat-shape. "But it's filled with my stuff."

"It's all we have right now," she pulled him like a cat on a leash toward the parking garage. "We can't end the night on an unfulfilling and embarrassing tryst. Not after our amazing time at Bingo last night. If we never see each other again, then I need to end whatever this is on a full-card, O-69 Bingo! Do you understand what I'm saying?"

"Yes, ma'am. Please get your dabber ready!" He picked up his pace and led the way to his car.

"That's what I'm supposed to say to you," she teased. He scooped her up and carried her toward the parking garage.

As he approached the car, he frowned and slowed. Emma wondered what his problem was, until she saw that his car, a shiny white Lotus, was stuffed to the brim with boxes and bags. She grew concerned until he propped her up against the driver's side door and planted his lips against hers again, pressing his need up to her hip. She yearned for him, but knew she wasn't going to fit with him in the driver's seat. She wasn't quite sure what they could do next.

Jake seemed to know, and took over control, pushing the waist of her pants down over her hips and rubbing his hand against her clit. She was wet and nervous at the same time. "Jake," she whispered, we won't fit in this car."

"This is true, but we will fit *on* it."

She glanced at the hood of the car, then looked frantically around the parking garage. "Jake," she whispered again, the concern in her voice overcome by the excitement as he reached his fingers inside her. She didn't know whether to moan or panic.

"What?" he said as he unzipped his fly, his cock hardening too much to fit in his pants. "I thought you said you were used to being discovered."

"Lola doesn't count!" she wailed, and he wrapped his free arm around her body, lifting her halfway onto the car in order to get his fingers deeper inside her.

"Shhh, I'll keep a look out, I swear." He whispered into her neck, driving his fingers in and out of her while his thumb brushed her clit. "Just enjoy."

She quieted and closed her eyes, still anxious but unable to resist the pressure mounting in her body. He drove two, then three fingers into her until they came out wet, and as she began to twist in mounting pleasure, he suddenly took his hand away and moved his body from on top of hers. She clutched at the car to steady herself and almost shrieked at the letdown, until she felt his tongue on her labia, pulsing in and out. She moaned loudly and widened her legs, feeling the bristles on his jaw rub against her inner thighs. Within moments she came, and no longer cared about the public parking garage, letting out a loud scream as though she were cheering for the Seahawks.

Jake grunted in excitement, kissed her on the thigh, and stood up, holding her for a brief moment before forcing her to spin around. She laid her breasts on the hood of the car and planted her feet on the ground, spreading them slightly to give him more access. He fumbled with his pants for a moment, grabbing a condom. The cold hood of the car made her nipples scream in excitement. Within seconds, he was in her, pounding his dick into her pussy so hard it made her insides shift out of the way. Now, she was quiet for him, squeezing him with her pussy but being the lookout for them. She'd had hers, it was time to make him go before they were discovered.

The sound of a laughing pair of females echoed through the parking garage, but Jake didn't stop pummeling Emma repeatedly. She could feel his excitement grow and didn't want him to be let down yet again today. If the women were going to encounter them, so be it. She squeezed harder and moaned softly, prompting him to finish quickly. At one last thrust he paused, pushing deeper into her as he came.

The women rounded a corner, just as Jake's body grew limp. He quickly pulled up both their pants for them but had no time to buckle his. Cheeks reddened and sweaty, Emma scrambled to turn around and make it look like they were just a loving, smoochy couple. She put her hand in her coat pocket and stretched it around his hip in order to hide his unbuckled pants, and with the other hand she pulled his face down and kissed him.

"Nice car," said one of the girls. They appeared to be in their late teens or early twenties. Jake kissed Emma harder.

"Get a room," said the other girl, and laughed at herself.

The first girl giggled and punched her friend, then they ran through the parking garage, chuckling at themselves.

Emma didn't realize how nervous she'd been until they left, and her body relaxed into Jake's embrace. He kissed her some more, whispering, "We would get a room, but neither of us have one right now."

She smiled sadly, remembering that he was leaving. She pushed her face away from his and put a hand on his chest. "It's Sunday night, it's late, and you still have a three-hour drive to Portland ahead of you."

He reluctantly leaned back, a gust of cold air sweeping between them. She shivered, forgetting that it was mid-

November. She was surprised that the previous ten minutes of body heat had kept her warm enough.

Jake removed the used condom. He found a garbage bin not too far down the wall from his car, buttoned his pants, and left Emma where she was against the Lotus to go dispose of it. She shivered again in the chill and didn't quite know what to say next.

Finally, Jake spoke as he returned to the car. "I'm glad I found you today."

"I'm glad I could give you a good send-off."

His shoulders slumped a little as he fumbled for his keys "I wish I could have met you a month ago, or even a week."

She shrugged and looked at the ground, moving her toe back and forth across the white line between the parked cards. "Just bad timing, I guess. I didn't think I'd ever set foot in a bingo hall on a Friday, and then again on Saturday night."

"I'm lucky you did." He picked her chin up and kissed her again. "Do you want a ride back to your apartment?"

She ogled the Lotus, but noted the passenger seat was stacked with boxes and *is that a cat carrier?* She didn't ask about the possible pet. She didn't want to know this man any more than she already did. "You've got too much stuff in the car, plus we're only a block from my apartment. It would be more difficult for you to drive your car around the block than it would be for me to hop across the road. I'll say bye to you here." At Jake's slight pout, she smiled forcefully. "Good luck in Portland." She turned to walk toward a staircase down to the street.

Jake grabbed her arm and turned her to him one last time. "Don't forget me."

"I don't think that—this—" she waved at the hood of the Lotus, "—would even be possible." She kissed him briefly on the lips and walked away quickly, so she wouldn't be tempted to jump on his roof and beg him not to go.

At the top of the stairs, she paused to watch the Lotus fire up and bolt by her. It would have been nice to take a spin in that thing, she said to herself as he gave a light honk and wave. When the car was gone, she paced down the stairs to the street.

CHAPTER SIXTEEN

Kier and Lola's bickering could be heard from the street. Emma thought briefly about waiting it out, but decided it would never end, so she let herself into the apartment as though nothing were going on behind the door. The fight was typical sister crap anyway, she figured. Perhaps her presence would be the thing that broke it up.

No such luck. As she opened the door, Kier focused her attention not on Lola but on Emma. "Oh good, here for another round?"

"Don't talk to her like that," Lola demanded. "This is her home, too, and she can fuck in it all she likes."

"Like I said before, this is Grandma's home," Kier stated, clearly reiterating a previous point Emma hadn't been privy to.

Lola's eyes rolled toward the ceiling, and she skulked to the kitchen to wash dishes. Emma noted the remains of a pizza on top of the stove. She grabbed the last piece, finding herself once again famished after sex and the stress of letting Jake go.

With the large dinner she'd had and now a slice of pizza, she wondered if she was stress eating, and looked down at her roly poly body. How he had found her so attractive she didn't know, but maybe men did like a little *cushion for the pushin'*.

"You should apologize to Lola," Kier reprimanded Emma.

"She did already, and it was as unnecessary then as it is now," Lola stated, bumping hips with Emma as she fumbled with the dishes. "We're sexual beings, Kier. You should try it sometime."

"What's that supposed to mean? Is that a knock at the fact that my husband is currently cheating on me?"

"Oh, for Heaven's sake, no," Lola said, half apologetically, half obviously frustrated.

Emma wondered how long she could stay silent while the two sisters argued.

Turns out it wasn't long.

"Where is Captain Bingo," Kier asked rhetorically, storming about the apartment and running fingers along undusted surfaces.

"He left," was all Emma got in. She longed for the chance to sit down with Lola and discuss everything that had happened over the weekend. She knew the opportunity would not come for a while.

Kier continued her rant. "You two have no idea what it's like to be married with a child. You're thirty-five years old and you should have settled down long ago."

"Yes, Kier," the roommates mocked in unison, a flashback to when they were teens and Lola's older sister would criticize them for not planning out the next fifty years of their lives.

Kier wasn't listening. She was adjusting the books on the bookshelf in order of tallest to shortest, rather than alphabetical as Lola preferred them to be. As she did so, she sighed. Emma opened the fridge to grab a drink and found zero booze but a lot of organic green juice. She waved it in the air and raised an eyebrow at Lola.

Lola tilted her eyes in the direction of her sister and shrugged, whispering, "She caught up with me at the grocery store."

In their mutual annoyance at Lola's type-A older sister, the roommates almost failed to notice Kier flop down on the couch and begin to cry. Emma was the first to hear the barely audible sobs and she ran to Kier's side. Not knowing what to say, she sat and held the woman across the shoulders. Lola watched and frowned but remained at the sink.

"You don't know what it's like to have everything lined up exactly perfect, and then have the rug pulled out from under you." Kier leaned into the hug.

"I don't, it's true," Emma agreed, not wanting to rock the boat. She'd experienced a little bit of it tonight with Jake leaving, but nowhere near comparable to twenty years with someone who decides on a whim to find someone else.

"He said it's been over for a while." Kier sniffed, "and that he was waiting for Tor to leave for college."

At this pause, Emma just nodded, not knowing what to say. She looked up at Lola who buckled her lips and shrugged, indicating that she'd already heard the story once already that evening. A few moments passed, and when it became apparent that Kier was neither going to stop crying nor continue her thoughts, Emma patted her on the back and, in a sudden flash of responsible caregiving, said "Maybe some sleep will help you feel better."

Kier merely nodded, and Emma guided her into her bedroom. Lola grabbed Kier's bag and rolled it in after them.

Kier took one look at the unmade bed and asked, "Have you banged anyone in this bed lately?"

Now it was Emma's turn to roll her eyes. "Yeah, Kiki, two different lawyers just yesterday. Do you want the side with the wet spot? Never mind, that's both sides!"

Kier flinched, and Emma figured it was both at the nickname she hated and the idea of sleeping in a bed which had just been fucked in. Quickly, she dropped the sarcasm and stated, "The sheets were freshly cleaned yesterday, and in case you'd forgotten, it's Lola's bed I've been messing around in."

Lola called out, "And I consider that very good sex energy, so it's cool!"

Kier sniffed and didn't argue further. The exhaustion had clearly caught up to her. She lay down and closed her puffy red eyes, falling asleep almost immediately.

While Lola shut off the lights, Emma grabbed something to sleep in plus work clothes for the next day, then they tiptoed out of the room. "I guess I'll make up a bed on the sofa," Emma looked down at the white microfiber and wondered how to keep her red hair off of it all night.

"Don't be silly," Lola squealed and led Emma into her room. "You're sleeping with me tonight, and you have to tell me everything."

CHAPTER SEVENTEEN

The women woke in a cuddly embrace, their legs intertwined like familiar lovers. Lola whispered, "Good morning, sunshine."

Emma opened her eyes and wondered how long Lola had been staring at her.

As though sensing the thought, Lola answered, "I haven't been looking at you long, I just thought we should start getting ready for work. We're sharing the bathroom with Ki, and she takes a while."

Recalling that they'd fallen asleep in a fit of giggles and forgot to set an alarm, Emma panicked slightly, bolted upright, and looked around the room for some sort of time-telling device.

"It's okay," Lola consoled her, pulling her back down to the pillow. "It's 7am so no rush."

Emma relaxed. "You're the perfect alarm clock, I should have started sleeping with you years ago."

"You say that all the time," Lola laughed, and slowly eased her body off the bed. Emma watched her move to the closet to carefully pick out that morning's power suit, holding shirts up against pants and scarves against her skin. It was a silent and methodical routine for Lola, born of perfectionism. Emma was glad Kier's genes held the worst of the disorder. She threw the covers haphazardly across the bed and sat up, stretching. Lola merely frowned at the unkempt sheets but didn't say a word. Kier would have screamed.

As it turned out, the battle for the shower would remain between the two roommates, as Kier was already wide awake and dressed, with pancakes cooking on the grill. "Good morning," she sang as the women exited Lola's room.

"I would have thought you'd sleep in," Lola said, grabbing a pancake and sighing over its delicious fluffiness. She gave her older sister a hug around the shoulders.

"I know, right?" Kier laughed. "I'm unemployed and my kid has moved out, but my brain still jerks me awake every morning at five thirty. It's relentless."

"It's OCD." Emma muttered without thinking, then sharply corrected her rudeness by saying, "Thanks for the pancakes, they smell fantastic."

Kier and Lola ignored the disparagement. Emma suddenly realized she was outnumbered, her disheveled and unkempt existence now being the extraordinary quirk in the apartment, rather than Lola's perfectionism. She made a mental note to clean up around herself more, and immediately began putting away the pans Kier had washed and dried already after cooking the pancakes.

Lola excused herself to jump in the shower.

"So Emma," Kier said as she fumbled with the newfangled espresso machine. "Tell me about your new guy."

"Oh, he's not really my guy. He's gone."

Kier took on an apologetic tone, "It's not because Lola mocked him, is it?"

Actually, you *did most of the mocking*, Emma thought but didn't say. "No, he moved away. Yesterday was his last day in

Seattle." She purposefully left the Portland part out of the conversation, not wanting to upset Kier who had just come from there.

"So you broke up? Yikes."

"Well, we were never really together," Emma said quickly, but realized who she was talking to. For Kier, one-nighters and short affairs were not a thing. It was get in, latch on, and ride it all the way out. *Now she's going to have to learn the hard way that nothing last forever.* Emma admonished herself for the thought, although in her experience it was true. She was so caught up in her inner monologue she forgot to finish the thought.

Kier stared at her, waiting for a continuation, but when it didn't happen she shrugged. "Well, I'm sure you'll find someone someday."

Emma didn't bother responding. The truth was until this past weekend she'd never cared to 'find someone' and settle down. It was only over the past few days that she realized having a sexy and intelligent male partner to use for dates and booty calls wasn't such a bad idea. She wondered if she could ever go back to one-night stands at the club again.

"You're in your head a lot." Kier was staring at her.

"There's a lot in here," Emma tapped on her noggin and played it off like the relationship talk was irrelevant, "I have a ton of work ahead of me today." She heard the water switch off in the bathroom and made a movement to exit the kitchen. "What are you going to do while Lola and I are at work all day?"

"I don't know," Kier said sadly. "Maybe I'll clean up around here for you guys."

Emma followed Kier's gaze around the room but saw no messes to clean. An obsessively clean person can find disaster anywhere, she figured, but she herself didn't know the first place to look for it. She was grateful for Lola coming out of the bathroom because she didn't have any idea what else to say.

CHAPTER EIGHTEEN

The bus to Redmond was packed and dull as usual. Emma and Lola parted ways at the Overlake transit center, Emma catching a Microsoft shuttle to her office, and Lola carrying on downtown to head to her job at a mobile service company. Kier had offered to drive them, having nothing else to do, but Emma insisted that it was out of the way and the toll road was a traffic disaster. It had been a half truth. Traffic from Seattle to Redmond was a pain, but truthfully Emma was more concerned about getting back to her routine. She felt different this Monday than she had other Mondays, and she didn't like it. She'd fallen for Jake a little bit, and she'd realized lately that time might be getting away from her, and that maybe she shouldn't live on her friend's sofa--once metaphorically but now more real everyday--anymore.

She wondered what it would be like to live near her office in the suburbs and do suburban things like bike to work or have her drinks at happy hour instead of last call. She wondered about school districts. Suddenly, the lifestyle of an old married homeowner seemed attractive.

She shook off the thought as she considered Kier, who'd dedicated her body, mind and soul to the lifestyle of the suburban domesticated housewife. *Look where that got her,* Emma reminded herself as she swiped her keycard at the entrance to her office building. As she stepped into the elevator with some other passengers, she was more keenly aware of their wedding rings, their tired but happy faces, and even a splotch of something on one man's suit jacket.

He caught her staring at it and smiled tiredly. "Baby spitup. My kid is three months old and can't hold anything down."

"I'm thirty-five and I can't hold my drinks anymore, either," Emma joked. The man's tired face brightened a little. When the elevator reached Emma's floor, she turned back over her shoulder. "Congratulations on the baby," she said, and the man's teeth spread wide in a proud Daddy grin that made Emma's womb rumble.

Work was slow and methodical. She was in charge of cataloging all the recent layoffs, some of whom were still searching for other positions internally, some who'd reported interviewing at other local companies like Google and Amazon, and others who'd already accepted jobs elsewhere. She began the day by contacting those still looking internally, helping them by sending them some openings, and making sure they planned to do exit interviews if they found something else. That took a good part of the morning, as disgruntled almost-ex employees yelled at her frequently for putting them in this position. As if she had anything to do with the layoffs. She couldn't quite throw their executives under the bus but making cuts in the company and eliminating redundancies were their idea, not hers. She just helped with the follow-through.

By lunch, the inundation of frustrated clients had her wondering if her ass might end up on the chopping block one day soon, as well. She opted to work through lunch to make it abundantly clear to the higher-ups that she was a terribly busy lady.

In the afternoon she decided to do the easy task, filing now ex-employees who'd found work elsewhere. She sifted through her pile and her eyes landed on Jake's file. She sighed in want, and took her time reading through all the things he'd done for Microsoft while he was there. The list was extensive, as he'd been there nearly twenty years. His salary and retirement contributions had been astronomical as he'd been made partner almost five years ago. *I guess he could afford dinner after all*, she laughed to herself. She thought of his Lotus and wondered what the price tag was on something like that, so out of interest she looked it up on the internet. As images of white Lotuses popped on her screen, she recalled the amazing outdoor sex they'd had the night before. She could still feel the chill of the car on her naked body, and the feeling of him pressing into her, holding her face down over the front hood.

An internal IM message popped up in the bottom of her screen.

        Paul Davidson: Hi, is this Emma Soledad and are
    you a redhead?

Emma wondered who the hell Paul Davidson was, and looked him up on the internal company server, learning that he was some principal developer in finance. A bunch of those people had been laid off over the last week, so she figured the message was something to do with that. Why call her out over her red locks, though?

        ES: It is and I am. How can I help you?
        PD: My friend Jake asked me to look you up and
    connect you over IM.
        ES: OK.

Emma had so much more to say other than OK, but it was all she could get out. Her fingers were on fire.

```
PD: Great, hang on.

Jakob Ono has been added to the conversation

PD: Hey Jake, I think this is the one.
```

The one? Her brain was spinning in circles. She decided to play it off by being nonchalant. It was her usual defense mechanism to cover the pins and needles that ravaged her entire body.

```
        ES: You told this Paul fellow that I'm the one?
I'm flattered, Jake.
        Jacob Ono: Hi!
        PD: There was a screwup. My bad. Apparently,
there are two E Soledads in the company. The last one
was not the one. She was a brunette.
        ES: Aw, Esther. She's a sweet old lady in
security; we get mixed up by strange male employees all
the time. :)
        JO: Sorry, my connection is slow. I'm glad Paul
found you.
        PD: I'm going to sign off now. Nice to 'meet'
you, Emma. Jake tells me nice things.
        ES: Nice to meet you too, and I'm not creeped
out about that at all.

        Paul Davidson has left the conversation.

        ES: You told your friends about me?
        JO: ...
        JO: I mostly told them about your boobs.
        ES: Great, now this Davidson fellow knows about
my boobs. That's professional.
        JO: Hey, your friends know about my cock.
```

Emma blushed at the thought of his sizeable cock and looked over her shoulder to be sure no one was watching this conversation. Then she remembered that the company is always watching the conversation through the back end.

```
        ES: Tone it down fella, or I'll get laid off
next for associating with the detritus. How's Portland?
```

```
       JO: Haven't seen much of it. Spent this morning
trying to hijack Wifi out of my friend's garage. Hence
the slow responses.
       ES: Your friend is launching a startup and
doesn't have Wifi?
       JO: Money was tight. I'm not only the biz dev
manager, I'm also funding it a little. I ordered
internet and phone but it won't be installed until
Wednesday.
```

Emma didn't know what to say at this point. Were they just casually talking like old friends, or was this supposed to mean something? Should she ask him outright what he wants, or would that be rude? She had no idea, so rather than embarrass herself she didn't respond right away, instead trying to focus on some other ex-employee documents.

A few minutes later, he sent another message.

```
       JO: So anyway, I'm glad I found you. I just
wanted to add you to my contacts list and say
```

His message seemed to cut off there, but a little icon showed he was still typing. She waited and watched rather than touch the keyboard herself. *Say what? Say what?*

```
       JO: hello.
```

Oh. That's it? Just hello!? Her brain was reeling, but she couldn't figure out why. This meant nothing. It meant nothing. He'd just been a booty call, that's it. And yet he was in every other thought and his silly little IMs made her heart flutter. She tried to type a million things but in the end she couldn't come up with anything to say, so she sent a simple emoticon.

```
       ES: 8D
```

...and immediately regretted it.

```
       JO: sunglass smiley face? That's nice. Thanks
for that.
```

ES: Hey, where I come from it means I love you.

...and she *absolutely immediately regretted that!!* But there was no erasing things on IM. Now that blunder was out there. She scrambled to type something, anything, to erase what she'd just written. She was sure she didn't even mean it. She'd only known the guy for three whole days and *Oh my god what did I just do?!*

JO: 8D Okay then.

Did that mean "I love you, okay then?" or was he just mimicking the smiley emoticon? Now she had no idea. She thought desperately of something professional and standoffish to say. In the end, she settled on:

ES: Anyway, these employees won't fire themselves. Thanks for the add. Have a Voodoo donut for me and keep in touch.

And she immediately changed her status to 'offline.'
Then she ran downstairs to the cafeteria and buried her embarrassed sorrows in a plate of vegetarian couscous.

CHAPTER NINETEEN

he rest of Monday went by slowly, Emma's thoughts reenacting every stupid mistake she'd made over instant message again and again. Although she did log back in during mid-afternoon, Jake didn't contact her again. Was he scared off, or just busy? She hoped it was the latter, but she berated herself nonetheless for her foolish and thoughtless post. "It means I love you?" What was she thinking? She hadn't said anything like that to any man since her 6th grade boyfriend.

She had trouble focusing on work, and in the end decided to cut out of the office early. She sent a quick text to Lola telling her not to wait for her at the transit center, and she set off towards the shuttle station to catch the express bus to Westlake Mall. From there, she'd walk and let the cool night air freeze away her ridiculously overzealous and naive mistake.

Unfortunately, the walk from Westlake Mall to Pioneer Square took her right down 1st street and in front of the restaurant they'd eaten at the night before. She paused outside the window to stare down the couple who were seated at their table. The male and female were each engrossed in their own smartphones and not paying any attention to each other. Emma wondered if they were a better pair or a worse one.

"At least you can't accidentally say 'I love you' that way," she said to the window. The male briefly looked up and gave her a cursory once-over, then went back to his phone. Emma left in a huff, still angry at herself but finding it easier to be hateful toward people she didn't know.

As she passed the sinking ship parking garage, she sighed, and the familiar rumble in her womb happened again. The sex with Jake was so amazing it had left a vacancy when it ended. Why couldn't she have met him a week, or two, or seven before? They could have had a wilder affair than just a three-day tryst.

In that moment, she realized that like most Seattle residents she hated that parking garage. It was a horrible blight on the cool hipster neighborhood that was Pioneer Square. Now she hated it even more. It possessed a memory of sex that ruined her for other men.

She stormed into Lola's apartment building, hating that too. She stomped up the stairs hating stairs. She threw open the apartment door hating apartment doors, and Lola's room, and the sofa, and anywhere she'd touched Jake the night before.

Kier popped out of her bedroom with a box of random clutter, waving a bingo dabber in the air "What's this?" she spoke to the object, ignoring Emma's frown. "Do you guys play Bingo?"

"No. I hate Bingo!" Emma stormed into the bathroom and slammed the door.

#

After a long, hot shower, Emma opted for a nap rather than try to carry on a conversation with Kier. It wasn't that idle conversation was difficult with the woman, she just didn't know how to be with someone who was going through a messy separation after twenty years of marriage. She also needed some time to be alone in her own head and regret everything that had happened over the course of the past few days. After her shower she snuck into bed--Lola's bed--and put her head down for a long nap. Although sleep came easy, it was fitful and not very deep. She'd had a long weekend and an even longer weekday.

Lola arrived home around 8pm, as usual, and Emma woke to hear her and Kier in a muted conversation. She couldn't tell if they were talking about her or trying to stay quiet while she napped. Rather than interrupt them to try and listen in, she made a point of creating noise as she awoke. By the time she exited the room, Kier and Lola were silent, just looking at her.

"I'm fine." She wasn't. "A nap was needed after that wild weekend, am I right?" She tried to smile as though everything was okay and it was all one big joke.

Kier seemed fine with her explanation. Lola's face told Emma she was having none of it, but she stayed quiet.

"Want me to make dinner tonight?" Emma moved past them to the kitchen and looked around in the fridge. A sting of tears burned her corneas, but she tried to keep her wits about her as she looked through their supplies. She saw chicken and frozen veggies, so a simple stir fry would do.

Lola broke the silence first. "So, Kier, what did you do today?"

"First I walked to Pike Market and bought some spices, and then I mainly spent the day cleaning Emma's room." At Emma's horrified look, Kier quickly interjected with an attempt at appeasement. "I mean, I tidied it up for you. I hope that's okay."

"Of course. Of course it is." Emma nodded. It wasn't, really, but she didn't want to rock the boat by freaking out. She suddenly remembered a bevy of sex toys strewn haphazardly in the bedside table and wondered if Kier had tidied *those* up. Knowing Kier, they were probably sorted from tallest to smallest.

"It's the least I can do, you guys have been so nice to let me come visit and stay here." Kier seemed to be unphased by

Emma's look of pure horror. "By the way, I uncovered a box of Grandma's old things. Did you know that was there?"

Lola shot Emma a look which could be read a million ways. Emma already knew not to mention Lola's collections, anyway, so she cheerily piped up. "Yes, we'd found them in my room, which as you recall was Hetty's room before it was mine. So, we boxed them up to make room for my stuff."

"Oh, good." Kier seemed fine with this. "I thought for a minute my baby sister was attached to more than just the old knick-knacks she has gracing the shelves in here." She waved her hand around the room, directing it toward the few remaining tchotchkes that Lola had kept behind, for ambiance. "Maybe we should bring them to the Goodwill or Salvation Army or something."

Lola's face grew pale, and she struggled for something to say.

"Nah, I think some of them are worth money," said Emma. "Plus, I like the memories. Hetty and I were close, too." If Kier couldn't deal with Lola's attachment to her grandma, then Emma would take it on as her own issue. Lola shot her a look of gratitude.

"Hetty was a crazy old biddy," Kier continued. "Did you know she only kept this apartment in the city so she could have affairs with younger men."

Anger and frustration grew on Lola's face again. "No she didn't," stated Lola, "and even if she did, she was a single widow for a long time. They deserve love, too."

Kier brushed her off. "Sex isn't love."

"Tell that to Brent."

At Lola's retort, Kier balked. Lola felt instant regret. Emma stayed quiet, not knowing whether to admonish her best friend for the comment or agree with her.

Seconds passed as Kier's face fell into both deep anger and sadness.

Finally, Lola spoke again, "I'm sorry."

Kier marched into Emma's room and slammed the door.

Emma gave Lola a flat look, not knowing what to say. "She started it," said Lola, and Emma smiled.

CHAPTER TWENTY

Cooking the stir fry was fast and easy but required a lot of standing at the stove, flipping vegetables in the oil. Lola joined Emma to make the rice, and they worked in relative silence. Within twenty minutes the meal was prepped.

Emma queried, "Should I knock on her door?"

Lola shrugged. "It's your door, knock on it if you like." She returned to the living room and plunked down on the sofa with another design mag.

Emma could tell Lola cared and that she felt regret over what she'd said, but in true Lola fashion she was stubborn and purposefully obtuse about it. Emma tiptoed carefully to her bedroom door and held her hand up to knock, but opted first to listen through the thin plywood. Muffled sniffles could be heard through the other side.

Emma opted not to tell Lola about the crying, and knocked lightly before letting herself in. In her room, Kier lay facing away from the door, her body quivering with infrequent sobs.

Emma didn't know quite what to do. Were this Lola she'd curl up and snuggle with her under the blanket, but Kier and Emma had never been that close. She opted to sit on the edge of the bed and put a hand on Kier's leg, just to show that she was there for support, not anything else.

Kier continued to sniffle quietly but made no movement to shake off Emma's hand.

"Dinner's ready," Emma whispered carefully. She thought about saying more but didn't know what. So, she kept her lips shut and waited for Kier to make the next move. While she sat there with her hand on Kier, she looked around her room and noted the changes Kier had made. What seemed at first like a simple reorganization made the space look completely different. Her makeup and mirror--previously strewn about her small desk--was now on top of her tall dresser. This made it more useful, as she could now stand to put on her face. A pile of unworn tee shirts had previously taken up the dresser space, but its location wasn't clear. Emma guessed they were in a drawer or closet where they belonged. Her desk was clear save for a pleasant array of books Emma typically dumped beside her bed. The place was organized logically, something Emma didn't have the brain for. She wondered how long she could maintain the neatness once she got her room back.

"I put my life into my marriage and family," Kier finally mumbled. "I don't understand what would possess him to do this."

Emma considered a bunch of platitudes like, "maybe it's just a midlife crisis," or "he'll come around," but they didn't seem correct, and she didn't want to lie. Then she considered insulting him with, "men are dogs," and "what an asshole," but that didn't seem right, either. In the end all she did was nod and mutter, "hmm-hmm."

"Thanks." Kier began to rise off the bed, straightening her shirt and pants as she got up.

"For what?"

Kier thought about it as she walked to the dresser and looked at her face in the now head-height mirror. "Dinner, this room, listening. You're a good listener."

"I have to be," Emma half-chuckled. "My longest relationship was maybe a year. I don't know what to say to someone who has been married for twenty." At this, Kier smiled sadly. Emma stood to open the door for them. "Lola is sorry, by the way."

"No, she's not."

"Yes. She'll never admit it, but she is. Stubborn silence is like her version of an apology."

"How you've been best friends with her for so long, I'll never understand."

"Same way you stay married for so long, I suppose." Emma turned the knob to let Kier out and followed behind her, then considered her words before jumping right into her thought. "You survive each other's quirks as long as possible, until one day you make a swift exit."

Rather than get upset, Kier nodded and went to the kitchen to get a plate of food.

CHAPTER TWENTY-ONE

Kier and Lola seemed to make up fairly fast--a gift privy only to siblings, Emma figured, and Tuesday and Wednesday came and went rather smoothly. Emma and Lola would rise at 7am, Kier had already been up to shower and make breakfast, then the two would take turns showering and getting ready and be out the door to catch the bus at 8am. Kier would spend her days wandering around familiar tourist spots like Seattle Center and Westlake Mall, or shopping for much-needed healthy groceries, then the three would meet up around 7pm for dinner. Emma did not hear from Jake at all, and figured it was best just to move on. She didn't bother mentioning her 'I love you' slip to Lola, as she knew her cynical best friend--and probably the sister, too--would relentlessly tease her about it. It wasn't that she didn't deserve to be teased for the slip, it's that she wanted to try and forget Jake sooner, rather than later.

Thursday morning the ladies breakfasted on delicious Denver omelets, and Emma posed the question, "What did you guys want to do after work on Friday?" Lola and Kier gave each other a knowing look but said nothing. So, Emma continued, "I thought we could hit up somewhere in Fremont. Go see the troll, shop for records we can't play, that sort of thing. Kick it like total hipsters."

Lola smiled. "That sounds like fun, but actually Kier was telling me she'd like to go to Bingo."

Kier interjected, "I know you hate Bingo, but Lola was telling me it was one of Hetty's favorite things to do, and truthfully I do want to understand our grandmother better. I think it would help my grief. You get it, right?"

Emma realized she must have been stunned silent. "Of course." Bingo didn't end just because there was nothing in it for her anymore. Sure, she didn't love the game, and playing it would merely remind her of Jake's strong body holding the microphone like it was a dance partner, brushing her arm and making her baby hairs stand up, and pushing plastic bingo balls up her--

"You seem distracted," Lola interrupted her thought process.

Emma shook her head. "No, it's fine. We have the dabbers and gear and everything. It'll be fun. Maybe we'll bump into Mabel and Lillian again."

"You *know* we'll definitely bump into Mabel and Lillian again," Lola said to Emma. Then to Kier she mentioned, "Lillian and Mabel were best friends with Hetty. They're good people."

Emma wondered how Kier could change her mind like this. *I thought she was disdainful of all things Hetty.* She got up to clear her plates and get in the shower for work.

At 10am, her messaging icon lit up with her first message from Jake in three days.

    JO: Hey there.

Emma stared at it for a few good seconds, wanting to say everything and nothing at the same time. She didn't know where she stood with him, or if she should just let him fall out of her life with the rest of the corporate lawyers. She knew she couldn't, though. This wasn't the same.

She started typing a few things, but none of them were right. In the end she landed on a simple greeting.

```
ES: Howdy.
```

It was pretty lame, but there was no coming back from her lameness on Monday, so it would have to do.

```
JO: Sorry I've been absent. Neighbor got mad
that we were stealing his Wifi, and we just got
internet this morning.
```

Oh, whew. A wave of relief came over Emma. She'd thought a million things, that she'd scared him away, that he'd died, that she'd die of embarrassment over the 'I love you' comment, but the one thing she hadn't remembered is that internet was spotty for their startup company.

```
ES: I'm glad you're back in the land of the
connected.
JO: Speaking of connections, I lined up at
Voodoo Doughnut the other day.
ES: and?
JO: and the donuts weren't really that good. I
don't understand what the line is for.
ES: It's a culture thing.
JO: Okay, I guess I've been cultured. You'll
have to come down and line up with me, so we can be
cool hipsters together.
```

Was he inviting her down to visit? Or suggesting that when she happens to be in the area she should drop in? She had no idea. She began to type "sounds like a date" but erased the word 'date.'

```
ES: Sounds like a plan.
```

She was not going to make any more presumptions about anything, and this time she was going to watch what she said.

    JO: 8D

OMG, what the hell does that mean? Does he love her? Was it an accident? She was about to ask in the most humorous 'I don't care about this' way she could, but Jake's status switched to 'offline.'

She spent the rest of the morning freaking the hell out.

#

Back to work after a barely-eaten squash soup in the cafeteria, Emma noted Jake's presence online. She waffled back and forth about whether to message him or not and wondered what to say if she did. She considered a bunch of questions, then finally settled on mundane small talk.

    ES: Besides donuts, have you had a chance to
    tour Portland at all?
    JO: Did a bit of apartment hunting.
    ES: Oh? Is the sofa in your friend's garage not
    going to work out?
    JO: He doesn't like my cat.

So that *was* a cat carrier she'd spotted in the front seat of the car.

    ES: Who doesn't love cats?
    JO: People who are allergic. Also, as it turns
    out, landlords.
    ES: Oh dear.
    JO: I'll probably end up buying a place down
    here.
    ES: Wow, that's cat dedication.
    JO: I don't own her, she owns me.
    ES: Where are you looking?

Jake sent her a few links of places he had seen that morning. Two were small one-bedroom condos in the Pearl district, which Emma remembered as a great place to get food. One was another small condo near downtown. They were all in the $400k-$500k price range, so she figured his severance from Microsoft must have been pretty good.

```
        ES: Make sure they have parking for that sweet
ride.
        JO: What do you think of the first one? I liked
it the most.
        ES: It's nice and the location is good, but the
500sqft space isn't much room.
        JO: Yeah, Jennifer might freak out.
```

Jennifer? She typed and erased "who is Jennifer?" a few times over. She didn't want to seem needy at all, but she had to admit a wave of worry--or was it jealousy? --crept into the dark recesses of her heart.

```
        JO: Jennifer is my cat.
        ES: I was afraid to ask.
```

Only a half-truth.

```
        JO: Did you think I was in a relationship?
        ES: It wouldn't be the first time I made an
error of judgment like that.
        JO: Had some mistress action, did you? Hot.
        ES: It's not as hot as it sounds. Not when some
asshole lawyer's wife puts a death wish on you.
        JO: Well, I'm sure Jennifer wouldn't go that
far. You'll have to meet her.
```

Was that another invitation to Portland? First Voodoo Doughnut and now meeting his cat... it seemed like the modern hipster version of meeting the guy's mother. She didn't know quite what to say to that, so she left him hanging there for a moment while she collected her thoughts and tried to file another recently rifted employee. When she looked back at her message window, he was offline again.

CHAPTER TWENTY-TWO

Friday was like the previous four days, although on this morning Kier and Lola seemed to be getting along over their sausage and egg breakfast. In fact, a few laughs could be heard out of them as they discussed their lives growing up and how different it had been being raised in different households. After their father died, Kier had stayed in Portland and married young. Lola and Emma were only in middle school at the time, and slowly Lola drifted away from Kier and her mother. After high school, Lola left Portland for Seattle to live with Hetty and attend college. She'd tried the young marriage thing to a kid, Peter, she'd met in 2nd year algebra, but they weren't right for each other.

Emma had followed Lola from Portland to the same University, although for her four years of college she lived on campus. It wasn't until after Hetty's death and Lola's divorce that Emma had moved in with her permanently. The divorce was almost five years ago now, Emma thought to herself.

She missed Kier saying something important.

"Did she talk much about me?" Kier asked this seriously, and Emma surmised that she was asking about Hetty.

Lola was careful with her words. "Not more than a grandmother does."

"She didn't approve of my marriage," Kier said angrily, then softened. "I suppose, in the end, she was right."

Lola curled a lip. "Don't say that. Nobody could have seen this coming."

"Did you divorce Peter because Hetty didn't approve of young marriages?"

"No," Lola said cleanly and without anger, although Emma could see it bubbling below the surface. "Peter and I divorced because we wanted different things." She got up to clear plates, not wanting to start a discussion with her sister about the proper way to be married. Emma didn't want another argument to start, either. She excused herself and began to rise from the sofa, heading toward the shower.

"I wish I'd visited her more," Kier lamented.

#

The workday went by with little fanfare employment-wise, but Emma's heart sank as the day wore on and Jake never showed up online again. She didn't want to be pushy, but the truth was she missed him. She longed to see his quirky half-smile and run her hands through his straight and silky black hair. She felt like a fool for falling so hard, but she admitted to herself that she had. This might be the hardest she'd fallen in her whole life, save for the obvious mostly-platonic girl crush she kept for her roommate and best friend. It was easy to be confused when surrounded by such beauty every day, of course. But now a different kind of beauty had walked into her life. A rough-hewn working man with muscles to the nines and a chest you could drown yourself in, who volunteered his time on weekends to help kids play sports. He didn't even have a kid!

"Who wouldn't fall for that?" She said this aloud at the bus stop. A few people looked at her but went back to watching for the bus or fiddling with their phones. She wasn't embarrassed, she just finally understood the stereotype of the crazy person talking to themselves in public. She was that person. Jake had made her crazy.

The 545 to Westlake arrived, and Lola had saved her a seat. As Emma sat down, Lola held her hand and leaned a head on her shoulder. They received a few questioning glances from the passengers, and one lascivious leer from a creepy guy, but for the most part they rode in silence.

As they passed the UW football stadium, Lola spoke "I'm enjoying having Kier here."

"You are? I thought you two hated each other."

"We do." Lola removed her head from Emma's shoulder. "But we don't. I think this trip of hers--the fact that her Mr. Perfect husband and her amazing housewife life is completely falling apart, plus that she has an opportunity to sleep in Hetty's room and really get to understand how Grandma lived--is good for her."

Emma considered this for the rest of the ride into Seattle. She didn't have much to say to it, except that she was a little put out of her room. Sleeping with Lola was comfortable and pleasant, but she longed to get back to the routine. She wondered if that longing was really because of Kier, or because of Jake.

Back at the apartment, Kier had prepared a light lemon chicken and asparagus dinner, which the women devoured. Emma had to admit it *was* wonderful having someone feed her every morning and evening. Although she resented Kier a bit for taking her bedroom, she decided it was a fair trade for the delicious twice-daily meals.

At eight thirty, Lola bounced into the room from a second shower and spun around. "Are we ready, ladies?"

Kier stood up; her purse already prepped to go.

Emma was momentarily confused. "Ready for what?"

"Bingo! Remember, that's what we're doing tonight. Kier wanted to meet Hetty's friends."

"Oh, I might just stay here and catch up on work." Emma invented the lie to get out of it. She didn't want any further reminders about Bingo. Not this weekend. Not ever.

"Nonsense. You're coming." This time it was Kier pressuring her. "I found all these dabbers in your room. I thought we could share."

Emma was outnumbered. She relented and paced over to her--now Kier's--bedroom and tried to find something to change into. She wanted to be comfy. She wanted to curl up in a ball on the sofa and eat Cheetos all night. Stubbornly, she opted for a zip-up hoodie and jeans.

Kier and Lola eyed her but said nothing. They were both dressed quite nicely and had faces made up, but Emma would have none of that. She wanted nothing more than to wallow in her misery, *not* visit the place where she'd met the guy of her dreams and then lost him immediately. She decided that if there had been a way to pull off flannel pajamas in First Hill on a Friday, she'd have gone in those. Instead, she pulled on her trusty hoodie and she said as much to the ladies as they left the apartment. Kier and Lola both laughed at her.

"I bet you could have worn flannel," Lola said. "You'd probably match Mabel in her velvet sweatsuit."

"God, I wish I had a velvet sweatsuit," Emma only half-kidded.

CHAPTER TWENTY-THREE

Kier and Lola twittered while in line at Bingo. Kier peppered Lola with questions about how many cards to buy and how to play. Lola, as though she were a pro now, encouraged her sister to start small with the basic nine-card pack. Kier was certain she could manage eighteen.

The shared genetics is clear, Emma rolled her eyes to herself. In doing so she caught sight of the office where she and Jake had experienced that amazing first quickie across his desk. She wondered who was using the desk now, and did they know she'd laid her bare body across it, screaming in orgasmic bliss?

She bought herself a nine-card pack, not intending to play much at all. She hoped Mabel and Lillian would be there to watch for numbers over her shoulder. Her heart wasn't in it.

Their seats at the elderly women's table were still available. Lola squished over beside Lillian and made room for Kier to pull up a chair.

Mabel stared across the table at Kier. "Hetty?"

Lillian looked at Kier and put a hand on Mabel's wrist. "No dear, that's not Hetty."

Lola's sister blushed. "Hi, my name is Kier. Hetty was my grandmother."

Emma took this opportunity to really look at Lola's sister. Kier's similarity to Hetty was so striking, Emma wondered how she hadn't noticed it before. Hetty, Kier & Lola possessed the same grey eyes and pointed cheeks, but Lola's lips, dyed hair, and more curvaceous body were a completely different shape. Kier's body was the same as Hetty's. In fact, her shorter apple shape and trimmed hair made her look almost identical to her grandmother. The only difference was that where Hetty's face was filled with immeasurable joy, Kier's possessed a level of sadness, as though the world had beat her down.

Kier caught Emma staring at her and raised an eyebrow.

Emma fumbled with her purse and muttered something about going to get sodas. Kier ordered a small diet coke and Lola asked for a root beer. Emma repeated those two drinks in her head so she wouldn't forget them.

As she approached the counter, she saw Aidan working the drink machine again. "Hello," she chirped at him, causing him to fumble with the ice. He dumped it out and remeasured it into the cup he was holding, although Emma noted he had no other customers. She wondered if he was trying to get ahead of his perfectionism by pre-filling drink cups with ice.

"Hey," Aidan straightened himself, attempting to look more mature than his 17 years. Emma's cheeks grew pink at his attention. It was flattering to get any man's attention, no matter how young. She imagined he'd make someone a great boyfriend one day.

"I'll have a small diet coke and a medium root beer," Emma ordered, taking five dollars out of her wallet.

Sure enough, Aidan used the pre-measured cup for one of the drinks. Emma mentally patted herself on the back for spotting his disorder and realizing what he'd done. The biggest pat should have gone to him, she thought, for coming up with a coping mechanism in the first place.

As he handed her that first soda, the cold chill of the ice made the hairs on her arm stand on end. She briefly pulled away from the drink as though it were poisoned.

The back of her neck tingled like she'd just been out in a snowstorm, and her legs grew numb where she stood. As her stomach flipped with butterflies, she wondered what the hell was happening to her.

Aidan handed her the second drink and broke her tension. "Jake!"

"Jake?" She managed to breathe out as her knees went numb. "What about him?" She threw the five dollars at Aidan and grabbed the two drinks, turning from the counter and staring right into Jake's chest. Now her body lit up on fire, and she squeezed the drinks in her hands. Root beer and diet coke went flying over her arms and sweater, and dripped down Jake's pant leg.

Now Jake spoke, "we have to stop meeting like this."

Aidan laughed and began making new drinks, carefully measuring out the ice.

Emma had no bearings left to collect. She put the cups on the counter and grabbed an entire box of napkins, not knowing exactly what was happening or how to fix it. Finally, she found words in her brain. "This isn't Portland."

Kind of a stupid thing to say, her subconscious screamed at her.

"It isn't?" Jake was half mocking her, but he slid a hand under her elbow to steady her.

She hoped he'd thought it was merely a clumsy mistake, and that he couldn't read the fact that her body was completely collapsing in his presence.

Jake continued his joke, "Well how 'bout that?"

"What are you doing here?" Now Emma was steady. Aidan handed her another drink, much more carefully this time, and with one eyebrow raised.

"I missed you," Jake stated. "I went to your apartment, but nobody was there, so I tried here first. Truth be told I'm glad you're not at the club picking up corporate lawyers."

"We'd thought about it," Emma mustered a joke, but saw that poor 17-year-old Aidan was rapt with attention and decided against continuing the lawyer sex talk further. "But I think I left a dabber in the office here last weekend, and I needed it." She said this nonchalantly.

Now it was Jake's turn to blush a little.

Aidan handed Emma the second drink, and Jake took it from her quickly. "Now now." He said, "I don't think she can handle double-fisting sodas, son."

"Well, well, well, look who it is." Kier was first to spot Jake as he and Emma approached the bingo table. Lola smiled at him but said nothing.

Lillian and Mabel's faces widened in delight "Jake!" Mabel was especially ecstatic, but due to her limited ability to move, she was unable to jump up and grab him in a hug. Emma saw the spark of energy in her, though. She imagined the woman was once a real go-getter.

Jake bent down to squeeze Mabel across the shoulders. "You two know I couldn't stay away from you."

"Come sit, come sit! Oh, I wish you were calling the numbers tonight. I'm always lucky when you're here." Lillian blushed at him as though she were seventeen years old and he was her lucky charm.

"I'm the lucky one to have this big cheering squad," Jake assured her.

Mabel shifted her seat slightly to make room for him. He pulled over a chair and squeezed it between her and Emma. Emma put Kier and Lola's sodas down in front of them. She'd forgotten to get one for herself, she noted. She could try to blame the arrival of Jake for her mistake, but it'd been made long before he got there.

Someone patted Jake on the back, and he turned. "Jake," Mary said, "I thought you quit last week."

"Hi Mary, I did."

"Jake, go call the numbers one last time," Lillian pleaded. "I want to win again before you're gone for good."

Mabel urged him on as well. Emma winked at him, trying to suggest that it was up to him. Truthfully, she liked sitting next to his warm body, but she realized a riot might occur if other patrons realized he was here and not calling the numbers.

"For you, Mabel, anything."

Mary smiled along with Lillian and Mabel, and she ran up to the microphone as fast as a little old lady could do. "Ladies and gentlemen, I'd like to thank you for supporting the senior's center and the soccer association. My grandson Aidan plays every Saturday and last week he scored a goal!" She waved to Aidan at the soda counter, and he recoiled in horror at having been called out on the floor. Emma chuckled at him. Mary continued, "We have a very special guest today, ladies and gentlemen! You thought he'd quit last week, but he's back for one night only! Jake!"

The crowd of seniors murmured and smiled at him. *He's clearly popular here*, Emma surmised. Maybe he was lucky for all of them. *He was definitely lucky for me.* She beamed up at the stage as he called the first number, N-32. A hush fell over the crowd and all that could be heard was the soft stamping of Bingo daubers.

Until Lola spoke, "What's he doing here?"

Emma saw no N-32s, and processed Lola's question thoroughly. "I don't know, actually. I hadn't heard from him at all today. I guess he was driving."

"I see."

Emma looked at her friend, who stared down at her sheet with a grimace on her face. Lola was clearly not pleased but Emma couldn't understand why.

"He seems like bad luck," Kier frowned as she realized she only had one N-32 on her eighteen cards.

Lillian jumped in, "Speak for yourself, newbie!" She stamped almost all of her 36 cards. Mabel giggled with her, which made Emma and Kier laugh.

Lola continued to frown into her cards.

Jake called B-5, which made Emma's face erupt in heat. She was sure that was one of the balls which had been stuffed in her pussy the previous weekend. Her body suddenly ached in agony, as though Bingo balls were the only thing which would please her ever again. She shifted in her seat to try and quash the desire.

"Are you leaving, dear?" Mabel eyed Emma's cards. *Speaking of desire!*

"Do you want to play my cards? I forgot a soda for myself." Emma pushed her cards toward Mabel, who grabbed at them, furiously stamping all the B-5s Emma had missed.

As she stood, Emma looked at Lola, who stared at her cards purposefully avoiding Emma's gaze. Emma stalked over to the soda counter and lingered. She had no idea what was happening and didn't care to find out. She ordered a diet coke for herself, and Aidan got to work counting ice again. This time, she let him do his obsessive-compulsive thing, welcoming the time killer.

The ladies played silently after that, listening for numbers and lamenting when they didn't have any. Lillian did end up winning that first round, a nice twenty bucks in her pocket. Kier was miserable over the loss, having missed it by one number. "I don't usually lose at games," she frowned.

"Bingo was never Hetty's thing," Mabel stated.

Kier flushed at the comparison.

"You look just like her, you know," Lillian told her. "We saw a bit of it in Lola, but you. You're a splitting image."

"Lola got Hetty's personality, though" Mabel chimed in. "Stick both of you together, and you're her."

"I miss Hetty," Lillian said into space. The games continued silently again, but Emma saw smiles across the sister's faces.

CHAPTER TWENTY-FOUR

Kier was lucky enough to win a small four-corners game in the second half, and collected a free dauber for her troubles, but besides that and Lillian's win none of them came away with anything for the rest of the games. Jake thanked the audience for their participation and again for supporting the charities, then he jumped down off the stage to approach the women's table. A few seniors from the crowd stopped him on his way to say hello or thank him for their winnings, as though he was the magic they were looking for.

Emma couldn't take her eyes off of him. Just like she did on the first night last week, she ogled the way his forearm muscles curved as he shook the hands of his fans. She watched his calves flex as he moved between tables to approach her. It was as if the rest of the world fell away and she was the only woman left in it. Her womb screamed at her to carry all of his babies and perpetuate the species with miniature Jakes, as soon as possible. As though he felt the same way, he brushed off a few patrons and sped up to reach her side.

"So, where's he going to stay?" Lola broke the silence with her query.

Emma began to open her mouth, but Jake had heard her as he approached and he jumped into the conversation. "Actually, I was wondering if you'd like to come stay with me?"

Lola frowned.

"Where?" Emma's eyes lit up.

"Yeah, where?" Lola's tone was abrupt. "You don't live here anymore, remember?"

"I thought I'd take you back to Portland for the weekend, actually." Jake suggested. "I can drive you back Sunday night so you're ready for work, and--"

"Are you kidding?" Lola interrupted again. "You don't even have a place there, either!"

"Lola, please," Emma tried to calm her down, although she still didn't understand why her best friend was so mad in the first place.

Kier was staying out of it. She'd pulled Lillian and Mabel aside to help them with their stuff, obviously trying to get the hell out of Lola's way. Emma appreciated her attempt to disinterest Lillian and Mabel in her and Lola's argument.

"Well," Jake chimed in again, "Emma has some great ideas about where to live and what size home I should be looking for, so that's part of why I'm here. I want her help. Plus--" He eyed Emma and winked. "--We have plans to hit up Voodoo Doughnut on our first date."

"I thought our first date was the seafood place," Emma said stupidly. She was at a loss for how to respond to Lola, so all she could do was say dumb things, she figured.

"Actually," said Jake, "It's more like our fourth date."

Emma blushed.

Lola stared at Emma as though waiting for a response from her. As though she controlled the universe at all. Truthfully, a jaunt back to Portland would be fun, and exciting, and she had a better chance of getting laid there than she did at senior's bingo with Kier and Lola.

"Yes," she finally said.

"You'll come? Awesome!" Jake was thoroughly pleased, not understanding that there was a subtext in Lola's consternation that he'd been missing. Emma didn't get it herself, either, but was happy he was unaware of it.

"Fine," Lola threw out her losing cards and collected her daubers and trolls. "Go hang with your boyfriend this weekend. I guess I'll see you Sunday night." 'Boyfriend' was said with a twang, as though she were mocking the sheer idea of having one.

Emma played with the word 'boyfriend' on her lips for a bit. I guess that's what he was now. Although Lola's attitude made her sad, she liked the word 'boyfriend." Despite its immaturity. It felt somehow real.

If Jake had noticed Lola's derision, he didn't say anything about her, specifically. As his Lotus ramped onto the I-5 South, Emma stared blankly at the disappearing Seattle skyline. They drove in silence for a while, topping out at 70 miles per hour. The drive was smooth and sexy, and Emma wished they could pull over and revisit that hood romp they'd had last time he left Seattle.

"'Boyfriend', huh? That's a word. What do you think about that?" Jake's query broke the silence.

"I like it," said Emma, flipping the word over silently in her mouth.

"Good, it's a thing then. We're a thing."

Emma blushed and smiled, but sadly. "Long distance relationships are hard."

Now it was Jake's turn to spin things around in his head. Finally, he winked at her and joked, "I'll tell you what's *hard*."

"Oh, is that so?"

She reached into his lap, felt around for his belt buckle, and gave him a hand job while he drove, but wouldn't let him finish while driving. He sped up to 80 and made it back to Portland in a record two and a half hours.

As they approached the city, it occurred to Emma that he was currently living on someone's couch and that there probably wouldn't be room for her. She brought this up as he steered onto the Oregon-Washington bridge.

"Oh, the team always has a date or two visiting," he said plainly.

"Is it just a weird frat house like in that Facebook movie? Do you all just sit around talking about coding, and girls come and go for the pool?"

Jake laughed. "No, we're in our late thirties and early forties, no one can sustain that type of lifestyle. We have two married guys on the team, too, who go back to do it at their own houses after work. Also, it's not a frat house because we have a woman on our team. Actually, she gets laid the most and we're all quite envious about it."

"So, you just brought me to stay competitive?"

"Oh heck yes!" He kidded. "But you're right, maybe we should get a room."

Emma used her phone to call around for some hotels. Jake began to pull his wallet out of his pocket, and she brushed him off. "You paid for our third date. I've got this one." She reserved a room at a Hilton across from Voodoo Doughnut so they could be first in line the next morning.

They would never make it there the next day, however.

As soon as they got into their room, Jake grabbed her and pulled her face to his, ogling the deepest recesses of her eyes almost to the point where she felt uncomfortable, then he kissed her hard, like a soldier coming back from war. "God, I missed this," he said as they both came back up for air.

He unzipped her hoodie, and threw it to the ground, her bra and yoga pants the only thing hugging her body. Once again, she wished she'd chosen sexier clothes.

"No, no, no, no, this will not do," he stated as he caressed her chest with his eyes. Like a bingo card waiting to be stamped, she quickly did away with the bra and pants, until she was completely naked and he fully clothed. He nodded approval of her, then looked at himself.

"That won't do either," she frowned, pointing at his clothes. He began to pull his shirt off over his head, revealing his taught abs and chest, and she almost swooned like a schoolgirl. She leapt at his pant waist and undid them while he fidgeted with the shirt over his strong shoulders, then she got on her knees and swallowed his cock whole.

"Oh my god, woman." The shirt got stuck on his head as his knees began to weaken. "You're amazing."

She couldn't respond, she was too busy devouring him. The more he grunted, the more excited and wet she became.

She prayed he'd stuck a condom in his pants and fidgeted for it in the pile on the floor. When her fingers found it, she almost cried in happy desperation.

"Emma," Jake half-whispered. She took this as an opportunity to reach up with her hand and play with his nuts. "Emma," he stated again, a little louder this time. "You got me so hot in the car, I--"

She faked a groan, as though his talking was getting her hot. Truth was, she was hot enough as it was, she didn't need the endorsement.

"Emma, please." he grabbed her head and withdrew his dick, a move that tortured her so much, she licked the tip of his cock as it exited her mouth.

He came all over her face, half exalted, half desperate. She licked and swallowed what she could, the rest dripped down her chin onto her bare breasts.

"I told you," Jake said as he grabbed her hand and helped her up. "You got me too hot in the car two hours ago. I've barely been able to hang on."

Emma looked down at her tits and smiled at her ability to make the man lose control.

Jake pushed her naked body toward the bed. "You're a vixen," he said, "you had me at 'Bingo.'"

"I've never actually screamed that, you know. Although I feel like I've won several times since we met."

"You're about to win right now," Jake grinned viciously, and threw her down on the bed, spreading her legs and kneeling on the floor. His semen dripped between her breasts as she parted her legs. Jake dove his tongue into her as though he hadn't eaten in a week, then lapped at her clit softly like it was a salted caramel. Before her brain could process what was happening, she moaned in excited lust.

He licked her and she purred, urging him on. He pressed his strong fingers against her and spread her thighs even wider. Emma let herself feel every wave of pleasure, running her hands across her breasts, squeezing her nipples and arching her back, as Jake devoured her. Beads of sweat formed on her brow as she reached orgasm, screaming his name.

Jake closed her legs like he was tucking her in, then moved his naked body up beside hers. For twenty minutes they lay together just breathing and cuddling, Jake running his fingers up and down her body, and she watching him ogle her curves. As the minutes passed, Emma felt his desire return, pressing against her thigh. He looked into her eyes and winked, and she handed him the condom she still clutched in her grip. As he prepared, she spread her legs again in wet anticipation.

For the first time in their new relationship, they made love slowly and deliberately, devouring every inch of each other all night long.

CHAPTER TWENTY-FIVE

Saturday morning, they languished in bed, naked and pressed against each other. The opportunity to line up at Voodoo donuts early had been and gone, and the line now stretched down the street and past their hotel room. They decided they'd rather spend their morning in the warm bed than out on the street. "You'll just have to come back next weekend," Jake snuggled into her neck.

Emma's womb spun, and she enjoyed the soothing softness of his breath on her neck.

Her voicemail notification cut into the silence, beeping incessantly. She groaned and leaned away from Jake's embrace to grab the phone off the nightstand. He grunted angrily and pulled at her body, but she was able to nab it and listen.

Her boss's low and monotonous voice loomed in voicemail. The message was merely "We have a situation, call me."

"Ugh," Emma whined. "Work problems."

Jake groaned into her skin. "On a Saturday? Now I remember what I don't miss about that place."

Emma kissed his forehead then pushed him off, walking naked to the window and dialing her boss's direct number. At his hello, she said "Hey, what's up."

Her boss, in his monotone voice said, "The lawyers just contacted us, we're being sued for wrongful termination."

"It was a rift; terminations happen all the time."

"This one didn't like it. Can you come into work and dig through files with me this weekend?"

"I would, but I'm in Portland." Emma rubbed her forehead and watched the Voodoo donuts line slowly diminish, one patron at a time popping into the restaurant. She wondered if her naked body was visible through the window, but she didn't care. Jake made her less conscious of her body, as though a few extra pounds didn't matter. She turned to him and smiled.

Her boss jolted her back out of her stupor. "Can you get on the next flight?"

Emma thought for a moment, her heart torn between a wonderful weekend with her amazing new boyfriend, or her obligation to work when asked. In the end, she'd split the difference. "I'll take a late flight tonight and meet you tomorrow."

Jake frowned into the pillows and mouthed, "Noooo!"

"9am, my office," her boss said, and hung up the phone.

Emma searched her smartphone for available flights, looking for the last Portland to Seattle flight possible. Jake whined, his naked body strangling the sheets in pretend agony. Emma chuckled at him. "Look, there's a flight leaving PDX at seven tonight. I'll spend the day apartment hunting and visiting Portland with you, and then you can drop me at the airport at six." She walked over to the bed to start rifling around for her clothes.

Jake grabbed her hand and yanked her down to the sheets, bracing her arms above her head so she was trapped. "I'll abduct you. I could tie you down here and never let you leave." He began to kiss her neck and breasts.

Emma giggled and let him devour her nipples. "You could, but eventually we'd both lose our jobs and this hotel room won't pay for itself."

Jake laughed and let her go, moving his arm under his head and lying on the pillow beside her. "Why did I have to meet you now, just as I left?"

"You say that all the time," she whispered, and kissed him lightly. He parted her lips with his and felt her mouth for her tongue, which she willingly handed over. At the same time, she let her hands graze across his chest and down to his hips, feeling for his dick. Finding it at half mast, she was pleased, and rolled him onto his back, kissing his neck and nipples, down his waist to his cock, which she sucked like a lollipop.

Jake sighed and put his hands under his head, closing his eyes and letting her take every inch of him. "You don't play fair," he moaned. "I can't say no to you this way."

She sucked deeper and harder, until her throat could no longer take him without making her gag. Then she moved up his body and mounted him, rocking her pussy lightly against his hips.

"I'm not wearing protection yet," Jake whispered, his eyes still closed.

"I don't know if you have any more," Emma divulged, teasing just the tip of him with her body, but not letting him in any deeper.

Jake groaned and fished around on the nightstand with his hands, whining. They had no more backup after last night's events.

Emma plunged her body downward onto his bare cock, feeling all of it push against her G spot and signal her body to orgasm. Her nipples hardened in ecstasy, and her brain cried with logic and reasoning.

Jake gasped in pleasure, and tilted his chin up to lick her breast, grabbing her hips and not letting her go. "Evil temptress!" he cried, and gently pulled his cock out before plunging it back in again.

Her back straightened in excitement, and she tilted her body further back from him, pushing him back down to the bed. She put her head back and cried out to the ceiling while she rode him again and again.

He clasped her hips harder and tried to speak. "This isn't safe."

"I'll jump off," she rode him like a horse, faster and wetter, her body crying out for more. She didn't know if she could stop if it came to it.

"Emma," Jake wailed. "You're so amazing, please." He repeated twice, "I'm so close."

Emma was close too, her g-spot throbbing as she bent her knees again and again. She ignored him "Just let me fin--"

"I can't--" He pushed her off and down onto the bed beside her, leaning over her just barely in time to pull his cock out of her. She whined, and he came on her pelvis, tickling her clit with his slowly softening dick. The cum ran down her hip to the bed and she almost sobbed, not quite having finished herself off. Slowly, she let the want fade away, while he laid his head on her chest and breathed into her chest.

"What the hell, woman." Jake said as he kissed her cleavage. "If you want a baby, let me know in advance next time."

Her womb sobbed inside her belly, but she smiled nonetheless. She adored having power over him, even when it meant she missed out on her own pleasure. She'd had fun giving it.

Changing the subject to try and forget the pain of loss, she tickled his scalp and stated, "We can either check out today--" she tilted her chin to check the bedside clock "--checkout is in ten minutes-- or you can keep this room for tonight and check out tomorrow."

"If you're not with me, I don't need a room tonight," Jake said sadly, and got up to start collecting his things.

CHAPTER TWENTY-SIX

It was Emma's idea to forgo Voodoo Doughnuts on this visit, opting instead to help Jake apartment hunt. First, he needed to stop at his workplace to feed his cat, Jennifer.

The home was a 1950s craftsman in East Portland. Emma recognized some of her old stomping grounds, such as the pubs near the Catholic High School and the wishing tree. She hadn't been raised very far from there, although her father now lived in Forest Grove and her mother was in Eugene.

The home was quiet, with only one car in the driveway. Rather than approach the front door, Jake knocked on the double garage door. Within a few minutes it opened, and a cat ran outside as though escaping a fire.

"Jennifer," Jake motioned to the cat, a beautiful calico, and it looked up at him through one orange and one black eye. Jennifer mewed and moved to rub up against his leg.

"She's gorgeous," Emma said, and reached down to pet the kitten. It meowed loudly but let her stroke its back.

"I think she'll like you after a snack," said Jake, and walked into the garage. "Hey Mike."

Mike, who must have opened the garage, sat at a desk near a door that presumably led into the house. Two more desks lined the inside of the garage, and in the center of the space was a single computer sitting on the floor.

"Wow, this is a lot different than the Microsoft offices, isn't it?" Emma moved to the center computer and noted that it was a Tandy 1000 from the 1980s. It also wasn't hooked up to anything.

The man named Mike watched with apprehension as she ogled the old computer. Jake said, "It's okay, she's a geek, too."

"1984 or 1985?" Emma asked Mike about the computer.

""'86" said Mike, now smiling. "It's an EX. But it has been updated a number of times. Now it plays music for us."

"We play tunes on it while we work," added Jake. "Mike, this is Emma. Emma, Mike."

"Nice to meet you," Emma held out a hand and moved around the old computer to approach Mike's desk.

Mike seemed nervous but returned the handshake. "Jake has told us a lot about you." His handshake was weak, and he quickly removed it to return to his computer.

Emma shot Jake a look and he shrugged.

Jennifer hissed. The door to the house opened, and a beautiful woman in nothing but a towel walked into the garage. "Mike, I heard the door and --" When she spotted Emma and Jake, she quickly sputtered. "--Oh, hello Jake." To Emma she smiled and held out a hand. "You must be--"

"Emma, hi." Emma returned the handshake, and the woman adjusted her towel to keep it on. Mike smiled at her, and Jake attempted not to look, busying himself with cat food.

"I'm Sarah," the woman smiled. A car drove by the open garage door and slowed down as the driver caught sight of Sarah's wet hair and soaked towel, which hugged her body in such a way so as to show off every inch and yet nothing at all.

Emma couldn't help but stare, either. The woman was gorgeous. "I'd better go inside," she said, and the men nodded. She retreated into the house and Emma caught sight of an old yellow kitchen, but nothing else. It was hard to see around Sarah's shapely ass.

"Does she work here?" Emma was incredulous.

Mike nodded but returned to his work. Emma wondered how. There was no way she could think after seeing all of that.

"She's our PR director," said Jake, now returning from feeding the cat. "She's also the reason I can't stay here." A comment which made Emma wonder if maybe it wasn't because she was absolutely stunning and he couldn't control himself. But he quickly added, "Jennifer hates her."

Jennifer purred into her cat food dish.

Emma said nothing but smiled at the opinionated cat. She tried not to be jealous, but truth be told she was happy the cat seemed to like herself and not the babe in the towel.

"So anyway, this is work," said Jake. "I sleep in the living room right now, Mike is my friend who got me the job, and he owns the house, and Sarah lives elsewhere, although--?" Jake became very pensive. "What is Sarah doing here on a Saturday at noon?"

Mike blushed and said nothing.

"You dog," Jake said, and punched him in the arm. "We're not supposed to sleep with the employees."

"We don't have a team of lawyers to tell us stuff like that yet," Mike said, but returned to his computer, smiling.

Emma laughed at the entire play, but took note of the time. "Jake, if I'm going to be on that seven-p.m. flight, we'd better start looking at some places."

"Right," Jake agreed. He surveyed his cat to be sure she was satiated, then he waved bye to Mike and escorted Emma out. They waited as the garage door closed to be sure Jennifer didn't escape, then they got into his Lotus.

"So that's part of the team," Jake said as he revved the engine "except for Bill, who is our salesman. He's traveling trying to raise venture capital. He and Mike bought the house with what little money they had, figuring it would be a good place to get started."

"And Sarah?" Emma said, sounding a bit more envious than she thought she was. She really didn't feel threatened, but her body language was betraying her. She uncrossed her arms immediately.

"She's great at PR. She's working on our Kickstarter project right now. Also—"

"What?"

"She's my ex-wife and *I* broke it off with *her*, so you can uncross your arms now."

"Of course she is," Emma frowned, but relaxed. "Let me guess – she was way too hot and you realized you were woefully mismatched?"

Jake laughed. "Nah, I wanted kids one day and she didn't."

Oh.

CHAPTER TWENTY-SEVEN

Jake's realtor met them at a condo development back in the Pearl district. She already had a set of keys ready to take them upstairs.

"Nice to see you again Jacob." She gave a sidewards glance to Emma but held out a hand, "I'm Carla and welcome to Center thirty-six."

"I'm Emma, thanks."

As they rode the elevator, Carla started in on a sales pitch. "The Pearl district is Portland's best neighborhood, according to the locals."

Jake rolled his eyes behind Carla, indicating that he'd heard the spiel before.

Emma smiled, but prodded Carla with questions. "So how many spaces are available?"

"They're almost sold out!" Carla beamed with pride. "You're looking at apartment fifty-six, which is a one-bedroom condo with a view of the river, and there are a couple of two bedroom condos on the top floor." Then she lowered her voice and whispered. "But they're *very* expensive. We sold one to a famous actor the other day. I can't say who!" She beamed excitedly.

Emma could tell the realtor wanted her to probe, but she wasn't in the mood.

"There are only ten units on each of the first six floors," Carla continued, "so they all get two-digit numbers. It's pretty cool to only have a two-digit number apartment."

Emma widened her eyes mockingly and mouthed the words "is it?" to Jake. He shrugged. She hated ridiculous sales pitches.

If Emma thought her apartment with Lola was small, this condo was tiny. It had a lovely view of the river but that was where all the value was. Upon entry they faced a door to the tiny bathroom, with a stand-up shower barely big enough for one, and no vanity. Beyond that was a living room and kitchen combo, but only one bedroom off of it. It was a bachelor pad, through and through. The condo builders had tried to give it size by offering 11-foot ceilings and floor-to-ceiling windows with the view, but with the three of them in there, Emma felt claustrophobic.

"What do you think?" Carla beamed, waving her arm toward the river. It was as though she were trying to sell them only on the view.

Jake walked to the window and adored the sights, but Emma was much more practical than that. *Could one even fit a couch in here?* She wondered. It only took her five minutes to scope out the bathroom, bedroom and living space before she wanted to leave.

Carla was still flashing her pearly whites. "Downstairs there is a full-size gym, pool and a sauna!"

"What's the price tag on this again?" Emma wasn't buying it. Jake was still ogling the view.

"Four fifty. It's a steal!"

"But what's the real price?"

Carla's eyebrow shot up at the question.

Emma repeated it again, even though she knew Carla was fully aware of what she was talking about. "It's a condo, so there are maintenance fees. What are those?"

"It depends on how many features you want," Carla said carefully. "Rates start at six hundred per month, but I'm sure a muscular man like you would want the full gym access, too." She pulled at Jake's taught t-shirt.

"Ah, okay." Emma said. *Yeah, no.*

As Carla turned toward the view, Emma got Jake's attention and bent her chin toward the door.

He got the message. "Well thanks for showing it to me again, Carla. I appreciate all the help."

The three of them squeezed out the door and Carla locked it behind her, saying, "Can I show you the two bedrooms upstairs? That might be more your style." She said this mostly to Emma.

"We don't have a lot of time for that today," Jake apologized. "We're just looking at a few places before my girlfriend leaves on a business trip."

Carla pressed the elevator button and continued her pitch. "Will you two be living together?"

"No," Emma stated this quickly. A look came over Jake that Emma didn't recognize.

Carla smiled brightly and continued, "Because I was about to say that if you were, the two-bedroom apartments are probably more your style. These bachelor condos are really for working singles. Sometimes the owners even have a family home elsewhere."

At the main floor, Jake thanked Carla again and she told them where to meet her for the next condo building to look at.

He and Emma exited the building, and he asked, "What was that about?"

"What was what?"

"You answered her question as though the fiery depths of hell would open up and consume you if you and I moved in together."

"Jake, we've been dating for a week. Not only that, but I live and work in Seattle! Also, in case you've forgotten again, *a week*!"

Jake frowned but played it off. "Okay, of course, but you didn't have to be so abrupt about it."

They walked in silence to the car, where Jake opened the door for her and helped her down into it.

She thought carefully about what to say. "I didn't love the apartment. I'm sorry."

"I didn't either, but I was trying to be nice. She seemed really excited about it."

"It's her job to be flirty and excited about everything."

"Was she flirting with me?" Jake looked incredulous.

"God, men are so slow," Emma laughed, and shut the car door herself.

The next apartment condo was a similar setup and created an equally claustrophobic feel save for the pleasant street and park views. As they departed the building, Emma finally asked a question that had been burning in her mind since the first place. "Are you having financial trouble?"

"What do you mean?" Jake asked, and waved at a Starbucks across the street, prompting Emma to nod.

"You're a former Microsoft executive. I don't like that I pried, but I did. I saw your departing salary, and both vested and unvested stocks. You were doing just fine. Why the small spaces?"

"You didn't want to look at the two bedrooms, remember? You're not moving in with me." Jake said this in a joking way, then added, "What about you? Why do you live in a tiny apartment in Seattle? You've got to be making bank at the old software factory."

"I like to save," Emma said cautiously.

"So do I." Jake narrowed his eyelids in an equally careful manner.

The two laughed at themselves as they entered the building and lined up for coffees.

"I'll have an egg sandwich and a Grande skinny vanilla latte," Emma motioned to Jake to make his order.

"I've got this," he began to take his wallet out of his pocket.

"No, I've got it," Emma already had her mobile app out.

"No, I'm out of food so my order is going to be huge. You don't want to spend that kind of money, I insist." He removed a credit card.

"Just order. *I* insist!" Emma forced her phone toward the barista.

"Fine! I'll have a triple shot venti frap and--" he fished around in the fridge "--three of these sandwiches."

Emma bent her lip.

"What? I'm hungry." He put his card back in his pocket. "--and you said..."

The barista had no idea what was happening, but she swiped Emma's phone and grabbed the cups and a sharpie. "Names for the drinks?"

"He's Stubborn, and I'm Employed," Emma put her phone back in her pocket. Jake laughed. The barista rolled her eyes but wrote down the monikers nonetheless.

As they moved to the pickup counter, Jake put an arm on her back. "You don't have to pay for me."

"You don't have to pay for me," Emma returned.

"We both like to save on houses, but we also like to spend on food. What does that say?"

Emma thought about it. "Is this a psychological experiment? Well, let's see. My parents are divorced and one of them got everything. Is that the same for you?"

"No, my parents are together." Jake's eyes widened "but I'm divorced, and *she* got everything!"

"So, we're protective of things that can be taken from us, but not of food that we consume. Boom." Emma was pleased with herself.

"You should be a shrink!" Jake grabbed both drinks as they were placed on the counter.

"I'd never last a day," Emma took the egg sandwich. "Too many sob stories."

"Like Human Resources is any different?"

"Touché."

CHAPTER TWENTY-EIGHT

he third place they looked at was an open house, at a ranch style home that was near and almost identical to Mike's.

"This is perfect," Emma gushed once inside. "Why was this not even a consideration from the beginning?"

"I don't know," Jake said somberly, as he walked from the kitchen toward the garage, "I guess I just have some reservations about home ownership."

"Like what?" Emma was busy meeting and grabbing the realtor's business card.

"For one, I'm a single guy buying a three-bedroom house." Jake came back in from the garage.

"Well, you have Jennifer."

"True, she does take up a lot of space."

"So, what else," Emma moved toward him to put her arms around his waist. She looked up at his stoic but questioning face.

"For another, a house is a big commitment," he kissed her lightly on the lips, then pulled away.

Emma let him, sensing his apprehension. She shot a smile at the realtor. "Houses are good investments."

At this, the realtor, a young man in his twenties, jumped in with his sales pitch. "This is very true! Houses in the Buckman neighborhood are going very fast, and Portland's population growth is estimated to skyrocket with climate change. It pays to own in the Pacific Northwest!"

"Is that so?" Jake's eyebrow bent and he smiled at Emma.

"It is!" The realtor continued, having missed the mocking tone. "Did you know that with climate change, the PNW is predicted to be the safest place in America to live?"

Emma smiled up at Jake, teasing the realtor where he couldn't see her. Jake said "I did not know that! Tell me more."

"I'm a bit of a science buff," boasted the realtor. "It was my major in college."

"Well, I'll be damned," Jake said. "Mine too."

Emma punched him lightly, indicating he should stop. She turned toward the realtor and charmingly offered, "The home is lovely, my client will be in touch."

"Oh." The realtor muttered softly, "this isn't your wife?" He looked at Jake curiously.

"Oh gosh, no." Jake smiled down at Emma. "I don't mix househunting with pleasure." With this, he put a hand firmly on her butt and ushered her out the door, thanking the realtor again and quickly helping her into his Lotus.

"That was fun," Emma smiled "but I should really get to the airport."

"Yes," Jake concurred, his original comedic demeanor quickly overcast with displeasure.

Emma stayed silent while they got onto the highway, but after a while she couldn't contain herself. "What's happening here, Jake? You're afraid of commitment to a house and yet you want me to move to Portland with you! I don't get it."

Jake pulled onto the highway 30 bypass leading to the Portland Airport, but his jaw remained firmly shut. A vein in his right temple moved slightly, and Emma could tell he was either trying to pick out his words or refrain from saying something he might regret. She was glad she was traveling ridiculously light. Having worn the same clothes two days in a row.

As he pulled up to the departures gate, Jake asked, "Do you want me to walk you in, or are you okay here?"

"Don't spend money on parking," Emma offered. Then, feeling bad for her previous comments she said, "I'm sorry."

"Sorry for what?" Jake pulled up to her airline gate and got out of the car to open her door for her, a move she circumvented by opening it herself. They met on the sidewalk, and Jake continued his thought, "You didn't do anything except point out the obvious."

"Sometimes I can't refrain," Emma said. "It is one of my faults."

"I hope to learn more of them," Jake offered somberly, and kissed her lightly on the lips again. She longed to be swallowed up into his heavy embrace again. Even, she briefly thought to herself, to throw him down right here at the gate and ride him wet and hard without protection and not stop until she felt his cum soak thoroughly into her womb.

Emma shook her head at the nonsense, then kissed him back, licking his lips slightly. He seemed to sigh into her smooch but let her go. An airport security officer waved at him to get back in his car and clear the departures lane.

Emma ventured, "When will I see you again?"

"That's up to you," was all he said, then he disappeared off the curb and got back into his car.

She waved, and the Lotus was gone.

CHAPTER TWENTY-NINE

On the plane, she sent a quick text to Lola.

ES: On a plane to Seattle. What are you up to tonight?"

LZ: OMG What happened? We're going to late night Bingo again.

ES: I'll take a cab there.

She needed girl time and if Bingo was the best place to get it, Bingo it would be.

#

As soon as Emma's flight landed in Seattle, she grabbed a Lyft and within 30 minutes pulled up to the Senior center, still wearing yesterday's clothes. Thank goodness hoodies and yoga pants were fine third-day attire. She had ten minutes to spare before the game began, and she entered with excited trepidation, surveying the crowd for Lola and Kier. She spotted them at Mabel and Lillian's table, just as she'd left them the night before, although in different clothes. Kier was in Emma's seat beside Mabel.

Emma bought her usual, the smallest strip of cards, and she bounded into the room. She pulled over a seat without asking, a move that disgruntled the men sitting at the next table.

"Well, look who it is," Lola stated.

Kier smiled and tilted her head toward a collection of Bingo daubers in front of her. "Sick of Portland already, are we?"

"No," Emma sat down and took a dauber. "I got called into work tomorrow morning, so I took a flight back."

Lola huffed, "You didn't get dreamy McBingobutt to drive you?"

"Why would I ask Jake to drive a six hour round trip to drop me off?"

"He did a six hour round trip to come get you from us, it's the least he could do." Lola frustratedly stamped her free spaces.

Emma tried to ignore the comment, but she was hurt and surprised. Like the previous night, she didn't know where Lola was coming from. The older ladies, Lillian and Mabel, watched the three younger ones out of the corners of their eye. Emma caught them glancing at each other a few times, but she, Lola and Kier stayed silent for a good five minutes while they stamped their free spaces.

Finally, Mary, now the apparent Saturday night bingo caller, approached the microphone. She nervously tittered over the speakers, clearly terrified of public speaking. "Hello. Welcome to Bingo. Thank you for supporting the First Hill senior's center and the South Seattle Soccer Association. My name is Mary. Let's begin."

Without an assistant, Mary had to spin the ball cage herself. The yellow balls clacked an echo into the bingo parlor, and Mary fumbled over the first number, calling "G-four-six" instead of "G-forty-six."

The atmosphere was more subdued than Emma had ever seen it. There were still a lot of patrons, but the ambiance was quieter. Jake's sexy body and deep, funny candor was missing and the guests obvious felt it. Emma hoped that business would stay strong for the soccer association, for Aidan. She looked behind her at the soda counter and saw him sitting quietly, staring vacantly into the popcorn machine. Finally, she was done staying quiet, she felt like stirring up shit.

"Are you jealous because I have a boyfriend?" She posed the question to Lola.

Lola stamped the next number, N-32, harder than usual, and moved her lips as though pondering her next thought. She smiled pleasantly. "Nope."

What could Emma say to that? It was done purposefully and with the intention of stopping the conversation from moving further, Emma realized. The older women smiled into their bingo cards. Kier watched Lola and Emma intently.

If she couldn't get a reason out of her supposed best friend for her ridiculously antagonistic attitude, Emma would be thoroughly pleasant in return. "Good," she adjusted her body position upright. "I'm glad to be back. I missed your breakfast this morning, Kier."

Kier beamed. She was obviously startled by the adjustment in attitude of both women, but she sputtered, "Um, thanks. It's weird switching from cooking for three adults to cooking for two, but I had practice when Tor left for college and it was just Brent and I--" She dropped off, sadly.

Emma quickly turned the subject back around. "Well, I'm back. I look forward to seeing what you whip up tomorrow. Let me know if you need me to stop at the grocery store on the way home."

Kier smiled again. "Actually, I was thinking of making these cinnamon buns, but I need some icing sugar."

"Oooh," Mabel piped in, "I have a great recipe that uses nutmeg. Do you use nutmeg?"

The conversation for the rest of the evening was only minorly stilted, changed merely by the suggestion of food. At least the women could all agree on food.

CHAPTER THIRTY

Once again, Lillian was the only major winner, pocketing a two-hundred-dollar cash prize for a full card early in the second half. She gave each of the other girls ten bucks for good luck. Kier won another superfluous yellow bingo dauber, but nobody else came away with anything. As the game wore on, however, Lola seemed to find her groove and enjoy the evening more and more, which pleased Emma. Perhaps whatever was bugging her best friend earlier in the evening had passed, she hoped.

The sisters offered to help Lillian and Mabel back to the Senior's Center, and judging by their question and answer, this was an act Emma surmised had been performed the evening before, as well. She was happy to come along.

Lillian and Mabel invited the three of them in for tea.

Lola looked back over her shoulder at Emma briefly, then returned her gaze to the ladies. "Thanks, but not tonight. We're going to head back home."

"Hitting the town on a Saturday, eh?" Lillian winked at the ladies. Kier smiled.

"Nah, this one has to work" Lola tilted her head back over her chin at Emma. "She's not a night-owl like you guys."

Emma had no idea what that meant, or why she felt a tiny stab of jealousy in her gut. They'd made friends without her, and seemingly fun ones too.

"You say hi to Jake for us, honey. We miss him." Mabel waved a walking stick in Emma's direction, then turned toward the lobby of the Senior's center.

Lillian grinned at the ladies. "As you can tell, Mary is not the Bingo announcing type. We don't want to lose business or anything."

"Well, if they cut my hours at the mobile phone company, maybe I'll volunteer," laughed Lola.

The elderly women were greeted by a nurse, who waved at Lola and took Mabel and Lillian back toward the residences.

"It's like they know you," Emma said as the three exited the building.

Lola turned away from her and headed south on Boren Avenue. "Kier and I spent time with them after Bingo last night."

Kier jumped in. "Mabel and Lillian had a lot to share about Hetty. I learned a lot about Grandma, stuff I'd never known before." She walked beside Emma, Lola stayed slightly ahead. "So, tell me about your whirlwind Portland trip!"

Emma's tension eased. To Kier, she related the stories of house hunting in the Pearl and Buckman neighborhoods.

"Cool," Kier seemed interested. "Did you know I lived-- I mean live-- in Buckman?"

"I thought it looked familiar. That's where Jake's work is. I don't remember the street number, but there was a Starbucks on the corner." Emma blushed. "Although in the northwest, that could be any corner, so that's no help."

Lola punched a crosswalk button several times, as though willing it to change faster. Emma could sense that she wanted the conversation over immediately. Truth be told, though, Emma was done with the frigid silence and tension. "What's up your ass, Lo?"

Kier made an almost inaudible gasp.

The light changed and Lola stepped out into the street. "Nothing, I'm just chilly and I want to get home."

They walked in silence for the next ten blocks, hands dug deep into pockets and faces cast down. Emma wasn't going to push it further. As they entered their apartment, she glanced around at the small space and wondered if she should assume she had the sofa for a bed this evening.

Kier yawned and said her goodnights to the women, then ran into her room to sleep.

Emma got two beers from the fridge and watched Lola stand by the window and stare out into the street. Only when the silence because too much to take, did she try again. "Are you upset because I went to Portland?"

As though the apartment was Lola's kryptonite, her defenses dropped and her shoulders slumped. "No."

Emma walked over to the window and stood shoulder-to-shoulder with her best friend. She handed her a beer, which seemed to surprise Lola as though she weren't expecting her roommate to be so thoughtful.

Lola tilted her chin and smiled weakly, and the two moved to the sofa to sip their beers in silence.

Emma thought hard about what to say next. She finally settled on, "What can I do to make you happy?" and instantly felt like the asshole spouse who'd just offended his or her life partner. She hadn't done that, she didn't think, but at the same time she did want to make her best friend happy.

"I don't like change." Lola said. "You. This—" She motioned around the small space. "--Was my rock. You and I went out every Friday and Saturday to pick up dudes--"

"Well, to *try* to pick up dudes. We were only sometimes successful," Emma pointed this out jokingly.

Lola laughed. "We were successful enough! We had a good run! But now you're--" Her mouth sought out the proper word. "--Attached, and that's all changing."

Emma was quiet. Wanting to get out of a serious conversation, she merely joked, "Men."

"Men," Lola nodded. "Let's go to bed."

CHAPTER THIRTY-ONE

ou left before I could catch you on Friday. I didn't get a chance to tell you."

Emma stared at her boss. This was not happening. She could not believe she'd come into work at 9am on a Sunday just to be fired.

"No, let go," he'd said.

A security agent stood beside her, waiting to escort her to her office to collect her things. A small brown box sat empty on her boss's desk.

"I can't believe I get a little cardboard box in which to cram 15 years' worth of employment here." Emma was incredulous. The saddest part is that it would fit. She'd never set up her office the same way other employees had. She was glad now that she didn't bring in a sofa and beer fridge like some of her coworkers had.

"Emma, I'm sorry. This isn't about skill, this is--"

"It's about cutting costs. I get it. I'm in HR, remember? I tell people this shit all the time. I told my boyfriend this last week!"

Her boss walked with her to her office and helped her move some of her random desk tools into it. The security agent was nice enough to drop back, almost to the point of being invisible. It was embarrassing to be followed as though she were a criminal about to steal secrets, but she understood. It was protocol. She did this all the time.

It wasn't as though it were unexpected, either. The company was doing so many cuts, HR was beginning to wonder when they'd be next. She'd heard of a few coworkers being laid off Friday, but she hadn't anticipated herself being one of them. "Did you lie about the lawsuit?" She suddenly wondered if she had a lawsuit case, too.

"I didn't. We are being sued, but since you don't work here, I can't tell you anything about it."

At this, Emma laughed, because it was all she could do. "All the files from the layoffs are in that box," she pointed to a banker's box in the corner of her room. She hadn't even gotten around to filing them yet. Someone else's problem now, she shrugged.

He thanked her as she double-checked the shelves and drawers. Nope, not much at all save for a few textbooks on Psychology that she'd brought in just in case. She'd never even opened them once at work. The job was *that* unexciting. When she'd first arrived, she had high hopes of changing lives and making people happier in Human Resources. It took a few years to realize that it was just a paper pushing job with little emotional reward. It had taken the next ten after that to get used to it and just show up. In a way, this was good. It was all part of the change Lola had spoken about.

The security guard opened the doors for her and walked her all the way out. She shook his hand as she passed through the last locked door and handed him her badge. She'd miss that badge, it was a good picture. To the security agent she smiled. "Don't be next."

"Vendor badge," he flashed his own badge at her. He wasn't a direct employee.

"Lucky," she said.

#

Lola and Kier weren't home when Emma arrived.

They probably thought I'd be at work all day.

Hell, I thought I'd be at work all day.

She looked through her small box of things and wondered where to put them. The desk in the corner of their small living room already had a stapler and a photo frame. The bookshelves had all the books and knickknacks they could ever need. Most were Hetty's and therefore Lola's, but Emma didn't feel comfortable adjusting anything.

She walked into her tiny room and noted how fresh it felt, how abnormal. Kier had been there a week and had made it her own. Emma appreciated the useful changes, but when she looked down at her box of old textbooks and random desk accessories, and then back at the room around her, she realized none of it fit. This wasn't her room anymore, not for now. This was Kier's.

Her phone beeped with a text from Jake.

```
JO: How's work?
ES: Do you have a place to live yet?
JO: No
ES: Well, I don't have a place to work anymore,
so we're quite the pair.
JO: Whaaat? I'm calling you.
```

Her phone buzzed and she answered it before the first ring. "Serves me right, doesn't it?"

"They fired you on a Sunday?" Jake's voice was incredulous. "That's low. I bet there is a lawsuit in there."

"Oh, definitely, but I think I'll let them go this time. I feel somehow unburdened."

"So come back to Portland. Let's spend your between-jobs vacation together."

Emma didn't know what to say, so she remained lost in thought for a minute. She knew Lola would be pissed to find out that she'd told Jake before her, and she'd be extra ticked-off to know that in the first sign of freedom she'd chosen to spend it with her boyfriend instead of Lola.

The silence must have been uncomfortable for Jake, she realized, because he coughed and spoke right away. "I mean, I could use your help apartment hunting. I never know when the salesperson is being honest or flirting with me."

"Assume they're always flirting with you. Always."

"Even the men?"

"Especially the men. Salesmen are the biggest flirts! That's how they get their deal. Listen," Emma returned to the subject, "I want to come, but not today. Things are weird here."

Jake sounded relieved. "Awesome, the invitation is open all week. All month, even. What's your plan for this employment thing?"

Emma thought about it but came up empty. "I really have no idea. I've been with them for fifteen years and have never done anything else. I don't even know how to job hunt these days."

"Welcome to the club, babe. Welcome to the club." Jake paused. "I suggest you take a few days to fully absorb what has happened. Psychotherapy is a good idea, too."

"You think I need a shrink?"

"I think a lot of ex-employees need shrinks." He added quickly, "I probably could have used one too before I jumped on this Portland thing."

Emma laughed. "Listen, I have to go figure out where to store my stuff, and I want to find Lola and tell her about this. I'll contact you later."

"I'll be waiting here on my sofa with Jennifer." Then Jake seemed to use text-to-speech, because the next thing he wrote was, "sunglasses wearing smiley emoticon."

"What?"

"Love you, bye." The phone beeped at her that the call had ended.

Emma stared at it for a moment, then laughed at herself. She'd gotten so worked up over the love and boyfriend/girlfriend situation, she'd forgotten that relationships can simply be fun. She liked having a sunglasses-wearing-smiley-face-emoticon person in her life.

She thought of Lola and texted her.

ES: Hey babe, where are you guys?
LZ: Just got done shopping on the Eastside, heading back to Seattle. Are you done work already?
ES: More done than you would believe. I'll see you at home.

CHAPTER THIRTY-TWO

O h my god, Emma! What did you do?"

Lola's look of pure shock was so genuine, it made Emma bust out laughing. "Nothing! I was just part of the latest round of layoffs, that's it."

"That's horrible, I'm sorry." Kier looked uncomfortable, like she wasn't sure quite what to say.

"It's okay Kier, thanks." At the raised eyebrows, Emma reiterated, "It's really okay, I swear. I have tons of money, I got a severance, the world is my oyster now."

After a night curled on the sofa watching Pretty Woman for the hundredth time, the three women hit the sack early. Emma and Lola woke in a warm hug, then Lola got up to start getting ready for work. Emma watched her smooth skin change out of her wet towel into a clean crisp suit, and envied her soft, thin curves and welcoming hips. She began to wonder how someone as stunning as Lola could be single this late in life. At that thought, her womb began to stir again, and she thought of Jake.

Lola snapped her out of it. "What are you going to do today?"

"I don't know," Emma smiled, languishing in the silk sheets. "I haven't taken a vacation in such a long time, I think I'll just lazily catch up on movies I've missed over the past fifteen years. I've still never seen that Pitch Perfect movie."

"Fun. I'm jealous!" Lola bent over and kissed Emma on the forehead. "See you, later." She bounded out of the room and out of the apartment.

Emma smiled and planned to sleep in, but as the soft smell of freshly made French toast wafted into the room, her belly rumbled. Kier, she remembered, had probably made enough for the three of them again.

"Morning sunshine." Kier's larger frame bounced around the kitchen with ease. "French toast today?"

"Hmmm, yes please." Emma smiled and went to her seat. "Thanks Kier."

"You can stop thanking me every morning, it's the least I can do. Your room is lovely."

Emma tried not to ask when she'd be getting it back, although the thought did cross her mind.

Kier began cleaning dishes and putting them away. "I'm going to go check out the International District today. Want to come?"

Emma thought about it. "I would, but this is my first vacation day in a while, I'd kind of like to sleep in and watch movies all day."

"Suit yourself." Kier put the last frying pan away then grabbed her shoes and her bag. "I want to hit the ID before the tourists crowd in there."

Emma waved goodbye. With the house to herself, she could shower and walk around freely, naked. She was looking forward to this. She began with the longest shower she'd taken in the week since Kier was visiting. Thirty minutes, the chance to shave every nook and cranny and scrub out all the toxins in her body, as though she were washing away her job. She wrapped herself in a giant bath towel and wandered out into the living room. The windows bore no curtains, so although she was free to hang out naked, she still felt the neighbors across the street might mind. Or maybe they wouldn't mind at all-- another thought that creeped her out.

She sat down on the sofa and turned on the TV to the news, muting the sound. Then she opened her laptop and logged in, this time to surf the web mindlessly instead of recording boring data for work. It was freeing, and kind of strange to just be lazy.

Her little instant messaging icon lit up. Jake was online. She wondered if he was working.

        ES: Hey, how's work?
        JO: Better than yours! The crew is out filming
    their Kickstarter. I'm just here monitoring the servers
    for them.
        ES: Fun, I guess. I'm not working at all!
        JO: What's your big plan for the day? Coming to
    Portland?
        ES: I would, but I'm too relaxed.
        JO: Yeah? What are you wearing?
        ES: Nothing.

Jake didn't respond right away, and Emma wondered what was happening. Suddenly, the phone icon lit up. He was video-calling her. She blushed and clicked the big green button, and her screen lit up with his face. Behind him was the garage she recognized from her visit.

"Pics or it didn't happen," he said to her.

"Well, hello" she smiled. In the bottom right of the screen she could see her own image that he was looking at, and she adjusted her position. In doing so, her breasts jetted out into the picture.

"That's what I'm talking about. Now move the towel."

"I've never done this before." She smiled at him.

"Gotten naked on camera? I'm surprised." Jake laughed.

"Oh, I get naked on camera all the time," she teased. "Just not in the middle of my apartment."

"You were getting naked at work?!"

"I work in Human resources! Boobs are a human resource."

At this, he chuckled. "You're still wearing the towel."

She obliged, setting the laptop down on the table in front of her and putting on a show of undoing the towel, first exposing her right nipple, then covering it back up again with a grin.

"Wait," he ordered, and stood up. She wondered if maybe someone was coming back to work.

Nope, he wanted to undo his pants. She saw his frame stand up and the buckle of his jeans come into view, then he undid them and dropped his pants, his cock fully visible--and hard--taking up the entire screen. She grew warm and wet in her pussy. When he sat back down, she teased. "Oh no, not your face again."

He made a motion to push the computer further back on his desk, so that all of him from head to *head* showed up in the screen. She maximized the size of the small screen and pushed hers further back as well. As he took off his shirt to expose his ripped pecs and abs, she threw the towel away and adjusted her position so that her full body showed in the screen, too.

"Ah, yes" he moaned, and began to rub his cock slowly, watching her.

She wasn't quite sure what to do and said as much.

"Well, what do you like?"

"What do you mean," she asked.

"When you're alone, what kind of moves do you enjoy?" he continued to rub his cock.

"Well, I usually like penises shoved up my pussy," she joked honestly.

"Mmm, I like that too."

"You like penises shoved up your pussy?"

"Yeah, that's right baby." He was joking right back with her.

She loved the humor, but now that she was hot and ready, she wanted to get down to business. "Tell me what you'd do to me if you were here," she moaned to him, and tickled her nipple.

"Spread your legs," he said, and she did. "Yes, that's what I'm talking about." He began to stroke himself harder, watching her. "Now touch yourself."

She moved her fingers down to her clit, and as she touched it a surge of excitement lit up her body. It was already too sensitive to touch. She whined in pleasure, then moved her index and middle finger to each side of the clit, rubbing the hood up and down.

"God, I wish I could shove something in there," Jake said gruffly. Emma watched him beat off harder and faster, and wished he could shove something in there, too. She eyed the living room frantically, looking for a dildo that of course wasn't going to be there. She wished she was in her bedroom near the drawer on her nightstand.

Suddenly her eyes lit upon the bingo daubers by the door. She let go of her clit, sat up and moved out of the screen to grab one. Jake whimpered, "are we done already?"

Then she came back into his view, spread her legs, and said, "no, baby, we're definitely not." She tickled the dauber up against her labia and dipped the head into her pussy just a little, to warm up the area. The top was cold and smooth, which made her body freeze up and her nipples harden. She grabbed her left tit and squeezed it, willing herself to shove the toy deeper and deeper.

Jake watched with anticipation, adjusting his body to get more leverage and beating his cock harder. He squeezed his own nipple, too. Emma shrieked in excitement and her pussy grew wetter, she was about to come. With her right hand she tickled her clit, and with the left hand she plunged the dauber in and out of her pussy, her upper arms pressing her tits together.

Almost at once, she came, and could hear him about to cum, too. "Oh shit," he whimpered, and fumbled with a box of tissues on his desk, grabbing a few just in time to catch his cum. "I almost ruined my work computer there."

Emma laughed and removed the dauber, but she relaxed for a while in her pleasure.

She almost forgot Jake was there until he spoke. "Damn, I miss you already."

She watched him put his shirt and pants back on, but she laid there naked. There was no reason to dress just yet. "I miss Bingo," she joked.

"Come visit me," he ordered. "Get on a plane right now, just like that."

"Just like this?" She indicated her throbbing clit and red inner thighs.

"Yeah, I'll bring the whole team to greet you," he winked.

Just then, the sound of Jake's garage door reverberated through her computer. "Uh-oh," she smiled, and closed her legs.

"Shit!" he said again, and she saw one hand reach for his belt buckle and the other hand reach for the computer screen. Then the screen blacked out.

CHAPTER THIRTY-THREE

```
    JO: That was a close one.
    ES: It was sort of hot, actually. Were you able
to hide the evidence?
    JO: Just barely. I'm sure I looked like a deer
caught in headlights.
    ES: You were caught in my headlights.
    JO: And they were amazing. When will I see them
again?
    ES: Now?
    JO: I wish, but the team is all here, working.
    ES: I should probably let you get back to it,
then.
    JO: I miss you.
    ES: 8D
```

Emma shut down her laptop and turned her sappy movie back on. She missed him too but didn't want to distract him from work any longer.

Kier arrived home around midafternoon and sat with Emma while she finished up *Harry Potter*, which she'd found on the TV after her romantic comedy ended. For the most part, they just enjoyed the movie in silence together. Truth was,

Emma didn't know how to talk to Kier, or what to talk about. All she knew of her best friend's older sister was that she was married with a kid. Now that her marriage was in disarray and her son was at college, she had even more trouble coming up with topics. As the credits rolled, Emma tried to think of something, anything, to talk to the woman about.

"It's a shame about Robby Coltrane, right?" Emma was really grasping at straws.

"Who?"

"Robby Coltrane. He died a couple of weeks ago. He played Hagrid in this movie."

"Oh. I don't really watch the news." Kier eyed her fingernails as though they were fine art.

What do you do all day, then? Emma tried a different tack. "So, how's Tor doing in school?"

At this, Kier's face lit up, and Emma was relieved that she'd struck upon a topic that worked. Kier began telling her all about first year college, Tor's boyfriend, how she didn't love the new romantic interest but was happy he'd found someone, and what discipline she thought he might choose as he entered second year. Emma let her talk and puttered around the living room, putting away magazines and pretending to dust the bookshelves. The one-sided conversation thankfully took a while, and Lola came home just as Kier was telling Emma all about her son's elementary through high school education.

"Hi ladies." Lola put her bags down and removed her suit jacket. "You're chatty."

Emma rolled her eyes out of view of Kier, which made Lola snicker.

Kier jumped happily off the sofa and moved to the kitchen. "Welcome home baby sister," she said innocently, but now it was Lola's turn to roll her eyes. "I bought a few groceries for dinner, I thought I'd make steaks! Do you have a steak pan?" Kier began rustling through the kitchen cabinets.

"Um, we have pans," Emma said. She had no idea what made a steak pan different than a regular pan.

"Oh, that will have to do, but I'll go buy us a steak pan tomorrow, so we're prepped for next time."

Emma mouthed the word "us?" to Lola, and her roommate merely shrugged. She wondered if maybe it was time to ask Kier just how long she'd plan to stay with them.

"I don't know if we need a steak pan," was all Emma could come up with.

"Of course we do. Regular pans work, but they don't leave those wonderful char lines on the steak the way they should. Once we have a real steak pan, I'll show you. For now, sit back and relax while I cook."

Lola began to undress and walked to her room to put on comfier clothes. Emma admitted she couldn't say no to someone cooking for her, so she dropped the conversation altogether and sat back down in front of the TV. She turned it to the news, a bit out of spite for their guest.

After dinner, Lola seemed bothered about something, and Emma figured it was Kier overstaying her welcome. That was bugging *herself*, anyway. She'd hope being nudged into conversation about it would make Lola ask the "how long are you staying" question, so she attempted to bring it up.

"Something wrong, Lo?" Emma eyed Kier, who smiled innocently and went about cleaning up their plates.

"No, just a long day at work." Lola grabbed the plates from her sister and hinted that she should sit back down.

Emma wondered why she wouldn't just come out with it already, so she turned the conversation back. "I don't think we've ever had three people stay this long in your grandmother's apartment, Lo. It's cozy." *And by cozy, I mean cramped.*

Neither Lola nor Kier took the hint at all. Kier grabbed a magazine and flipped through it, while Lola piled the dishes in the sink. Emma took that as a hint that she was supposed to be washing them, so she got up and moved to the kitchen. Lola grabbed a towel but stood there with it, rather than drying the dishes. She seemed lost in thought.

"What's going on, Lola? You're not yourself."

"Nothing. It was just a long bus ride home and I'm tired."

Kier piped up from the table. "You poor thing, come here and have a seat. There's another Harry Potter movie starting. Did you know that big guy died?"

Emma rolled her eyes, but only she knew it. Lola and Kier curled on the couch as the opening credits began. Emma busied herself washing up the dishes, then called it an early night and went to bed. She never heard Lola come in the room.

Unemployment was exhausting and living in a small apartment with two other women even more so. She passed right out.

#

Lola *had* come to bed at some point, however, as Emma awoke with her arms curled around her best friend. She lay there spooning her for a few good minutes, just smelling Lola's hair and feeling her soft skin. She wished it were harder, rougher skin, that of a male. She wished Lola were Jake.

At this thought, she crawled slowly out of bed so as to not disturb her best friend, and tip-toed out of the room.

Kier was already up, preparing breakfast. "You're up early," she bubbled from the kitchen.

Maybe it was finally time to get down to business and figure out what the deal was. Emma said, "I know, it's surprising considering I'm on involuntary vacation. My question is, you're on vacation, why are *you* up early every day, Kier?"

Kier forced her eyebrows into thought, but Emma could see sadness behind her eyes, too. "Habit, I guess. Four years of Tor getting up at 5am for basketball practice starts to turn your circadian rhythm around. Now I can't help but be up by 5:30 every day."

"But you go to bed at our late hour, too." Emma helped by getting the eggs out of the fridge, even though she didn't have any idea what they were having for breakfast, nor even how to make it.

"Again, late nights with a teenager. They train you to go to bed late and wake up early."

"I don't know how you do it," Emma said honestly. "I couldn't go without sleep."

"Moms just do," Kier responded.

"You're good at taking care of people."

"Thanks. Why don't you start the coffee machine? I don't know how these newfangled devices work."

Emma laughed, but also wondered if Kier would have been able to work Hetty's old machine at all, either. As she opened a new package of fresh coffee, obviously a purchase Kier had made the day before, she thought about how nice it was to have Kier here, despite losing her room to the visitor. She was torn between wanting her space back and being perfectly content to wake up to fresh breakfast every day.

Her mind flashed to Jake. She wouldn't mind a fresh pot of *him* every morning, either.

As though Kier had heard her thoughts, she asked, "So, how's your boyfriend?"

"Good, I guess." Emma didn't want to talk about him, because when she did, her belly ached.

"Do you miss him?"

"I'm nearly thirty-six years old, I don't miss men." Emma huffed. Thirty-five years of staunch feminism and singlehood tried their best to push through what her uterus was screaming at her.

"Ah, so you miss him."

"You must miss Brent," Emma stated a little too quickly.

At this, Kier's face fell a bit, but Emma could see the feminist stoicism in her, too. Kier said, "I miss waking up with someone. I *don't* miss being taken advantage of."

"I'm sorry, I didn't mean to--"

"It's okay," Kier assured her. "I can tell you're getting bored with being displaced. If you want, I'll switch to the couch."

"No, it's not that. I love sleeping with your sister," Emma interjected quickly, "I mean, I don't mind sharing a--"

"I get it," Kier laughed. "And I'm sorry. I don't know what my plan is. My entire world fell apart when I discovered the affair. Truth is, I don't know what I miss more, Brent or the idea of Brent."

Emma nodded, but truthfully, she had no idea what those emotions meant. She'd never been in a serious long-term relationship. She started the coffee and the machine whirred to life, fizzing and bubbling with heat. She stared into it while it dripped slowly into the carafe, but she didn't know what else to say.

Thankfully, Lola ended the silence by padding out of her room and greeting the women.

"Omelets today," Kier chirped from the stove, as though nothing had happened. Emma gathered plates and helped her, wondering if she was angry or not.

As Lola passed by and went into the bathroom, Kier turned to Emma. "I'm only going to say this once. Love hurts but it's awesome. Don't be afraid to love, no matter how hard it ends up becoming."

"Oh, it's *hard* alright," Emma lamented.

Kier laughed.

CHAPTER THIRTY-FOUR

Emma found herself twiddling her thumbs with nervous energy. Where Monday, her first day after losing her job, was relaxing and like a vacation, Tuesday brought worry and boredom. It was a strange mix. She had money, plenty of it, as Lola's grandmother's apartment was fully paid off and therefore required very little in the way of fees and utilities. She'd been able to save her income over the years, but she was worried about what the future held for her. Did she have enough to fully retire at thirty-six? She didn't think so. She'd spent a lot on clothes, dinners out, and drinks required to sleep with whatever corporate lawyer she happened to snag over the years. With a boyfriend now, at least the primping required to pick up a lawyer was gone. She sent a message to Jake.

        ES: Just wanted to say thanks.

A response didn't come right away. She figured he was busy at work, so she flipped the channels to hopefully find another romantic comedy with which to take her mind off her predicament. Halfway through *Love, Actually*, her laptop pinged.

```
JO: What for?
ES: Saving me money.
JO: No problem. Explain, please.
ES: With you three hours away, and my no longer
needing to doll up to pick up corporate lawyers, I can
save money on makeup and clothes.
JO: You can save on those things even when
you're near me, you know. I like you naked.
ES: 8->
JO: What's that emoticon? I love you more than?
ES: No, that's me naked lying on my side.
JO: Woaaah, hot.
```

The apartment buzzer rang, and Emma set her laptop down and scrambled to reach the speaker.

"Hello?"

"UPS delivery for Ki- Kire?" the delivery man struggled with the name, drawing out extra syllables.

"Okay, come on up." Emma pressed the unlock button. Kier? It must be something from Amazon she'd had delivered. Kier was out again today, visiting the Boeing Museum of Flight. Once again, Emma had turned her down when she'd invited her, but was now wishing she'd gone. At least it would have been something to do with all of her nervous energy.

She opened the door as the UPS man rounded the corner with a giant box. Although huge and bulky, it wasn't astronomically heavy. She signed for it and set it down on the floor, staring at it.

Should I open it?

She went to shut the door behind the delivery man, but he stopped her. "Wait, there's more."

"More?" What was this? Where was it supposed to go? She looked around her apartment as he returned to his truck, then she peered down at the return address. It was her house in Portland, she surmised.

She pushed at the box with her foot, and it shuffled across the floor awkwardly. It felt like clothes. Maybe Kier was shipping her clothes to the apartment. She had arrived with only a small duffel, after all.

The UPS man delivered three more huge boxes, similar weight and feel. "Is this her whole wardrobe?" Emma asked rhetorically. The delivery man shrugged and thanked her for her business.

For a good two minutes she stood staring at the boxes now taking up most of the living room. She could be nice and move them to Kier's--*No, it's my*--room, or she'd just leave them. She opted to just leave them, mostly out of spite. She had no clue how Kier planned to share *her* closet.

"There's certainly not enough space for that in *my* room" she said to no one. She sulked back over to the sofa.

#

Lola arrived home before Kier, and although she noticed the large boxes taking up the living room, she didn't offer much in the way of interest except to add "that's my sister for you."

Emma was busying herself in the kitchen, having decided that tonight would be her night for dinner. Of course the only thing she knew how to cook was stir fry, so she was standing over a single pan with chicken frying.

"What's in those, do you think?"

"Stuff to make the apartment better, I'm sure," Lola hugged Emma around the neck and padded to her room to remove her work clothes.

Emma grabbed two beers from the fridge and opened them, putting one on the counter for Lola when she returned. *Stuff to make the apartment better? My apartment is already the best.*

Lola came back out in her PJs, took the beer, sniffed the meat cooking and smiled her approval, then went to the couch to surf through decor magazines.

"How was your day?" Emma was bored of the silence, having suffered it all day save for the UPS man.

"Same old, same old." Lola was not helping her out, here.

Emma dumped a bunch of frozen vegetables over the chicken, added a cup of broth and a dash of soy sauce, and threw a lid over it to let the whole thing cook itself. Stir fry was the only thing she could cook, but admittedly she didn't do it very well, either. It was more like stir-steam. She went to the couch to sit beside Lola.

"Is Kier moving in?"

"Maybe. I don't know, I haven't spoken to her much. You've probably talked to her more than I have."

"She offered to move to the couch for me, so I could have my room back."

Lola paused between page flips but kept her eyes on the magazine. "Are you going to take her up on that?"

"No, I thought we had a good thing going."

Lola didn't speak, but turned the pages more and sipped her beer, as though using it as a muting device for herself. Emma sipped hers too and waited for Lola to say something.

"Good," was all the roommate offered.

Emma thought for a while about how crowded the apartment was with three people, and how Jake had offered for her to come stay with him for a bit. She had all this layoff time on her hands, maybe she should.

"Jake invited me down."

Now Lola closed the magazine forcefully, but composed herself and smiled. "Of course he did, are you going?"

"Well, I have all this free time now, so..."

"I thought you'd spend it with my sister, visiting the museums and things."

Emma was puzzled. Lola had never made any previous hint that she wanted Kier and Emma to become besties. She didn't really know what to say. "I've seen those things and wanted a bit of time to figure out what I want to do next."

"And have you figured it out, then? You're going to go down and hang out with the bingo caller?"

"Hey, I--"

Just then, the lock on the door turned and Kier walked in. Lola had given her a key at some point, Emma noted. Kier saw the boxes and exclaimed excitedly, "Oh good, they came!"

Lola picked the magazine back up and focused on it, although Emma could tell she was looking at nothing.

"What came?" Emma asked.

"My curtains. I thought this place could use some, so the law firm across the road wouldn't be staring at your boobs all the time."

"You're decorating now?" Emma was stunned.

Kier went to her room to drop off her things and change into comfier clothes. As she passed the kitchen her nose turned up and she huffed.

"She's decorating now?" Emma whispered again to Lola, who merely shrugged.

When Kier came out of her room, she opened the boxes one at a time. The first one contained curtains, as she'd said.

Emma relaxed a bit. "What curtains are those, Ki? Did you order them on Amazon?"

Kier frowned at the nickname but continued her excited search through the boxes. "No, these are from my bedroom in Portland. I had a friend box some stuff up and send them only a couple of days after getting here. These windows are so large, they need fixtures." Kier motioned at the wide windows.

"I like the large empty windows. It's one of my favorite features in this apartment," Emma said quietly and looked at Lola. She knew it was one of Lola's favorite things, too. "Are these all filled with curtains?"

"No, some are couch pillows, and some are more clothes. I thought I'd dress the place up a bit, as well as myself."

Emma looked around their home. Antique furnishings abounded, and she thought it was enough. She said as much. "You're going to change Hetty's design."

"She's been gone several years. It's time for my sister to change things up a bit," Kier smiled.

Emma took another look at Lola, who rolled her eyes and shrugged surrender as well. Emma couldn't take it anymore. She stood up from the couch, stomped to the stove to double check the stir-fry, then skulked into her--*no Lola's*-- bedroom, and fired up her laptop.

```
ES: Want a visitor?
JO: Yes!
ES: I'll be there tomorrow. Taking the first bus
out of here.
JO: I'll pick you up at the greyhound station.
Text me when you've arrived. I have amazing news!
ES: Tell me now.
JO: I'll show you tomorrow.
ES: I've already seen your penis. It's not news,
but it is amazing.
JO: I don't know how to take that.
ES: 8D
JO: 8D
```

Emma, feeling much lighter and happier, walked more calmly out of the room and announced her plans. "I'm going to see Jake tomorrow."

Kier, happy and unaware of her gross intrusion on their lives, chirped, "Exciting! Can I give you a lift anywhere?"

Lola threw down her magazine and stood up angrily, catching Kier off guard and causing her to drop a pillow. She wailed, "So that's it? You're pissed off at me so you're just going to bail?"

Now Emma was taken aback. She stepped backwards and stumbled against a box, composing herself just as Lola started screaming again.

"Fine! Go visit Jake. Jake..." She began playing with his name on her mouth. "Ono. Jacob Ono. Yakob. Yako. Yoko Ono. He's Yoko Ono and he's breaking up the Beatles!"

Emma smirked and rolled her eyes. "That's kind of a stretch, don't you think?"

"No, I don't think that at all! I thought we were fine here," Lola stammered.

"Lo," Kier attempted to calm her down. "I can put the pillows away, if you'd like."

"Yes," Emma waved at the pillows. "Maybe that'd be a good idea."

"This is not about Kier's pillows! Kier can do what she likes. But this is *our* apartment. You and me. We live here together. I thought we were doing well just hanging out and fucking lawyers--" At Lola's curse word, Kier cringed but continued to unbox the furnishings. Lola continued, "--but then some boyfriend came in and screwed it all up."

Emma was dumbfounded, then noted steam rising in the kitchen. She walked to the pot and lifted the lid, sending a burning trail of water into her face. Calmly, she put the lid down and began turning the veggies, thinking of what to say next. "Is this about sex? Do you want to go pick up lawyers?"

"No, I do not want to go pick up lawyers!!" Lola stomped into her room, slamming the door behind her.

Kier arose from the third box. "I just think she's going to miss you." She stole a glance back at Lola's room, then determined it was safe. "A lot."

Emma felt bad but couldn't think of what to say, so she shrugged and began dishing the stir fry into bowls. "I don't have to go away for long, I was just frustrated about not having my room." At Kier's look of embarrassment, she quickly added, "I'm sorry, not that I don't want you here. I just felt I was out of place momentarily."

"Go be with your boyfriend tomorrow. I'll talk to her while you're away. Maybe I'll even take her out to pick up some lawyers."

Emma laughed. "I think she could use that."

"I think she *definitely* could use that." Kier took the bowls of food and placed them on the table, then went to Lola's room to try and coerce her sister out.

The women ate in relative silence, save for some small talk about Kier's adventures at the museum and around Seattle. Suddenly Emma was grateful for the third wheel. She couldn't recall ever fighting like this with Lola, but she was glad to have Kier to prevent it from getting worse.

CHAPTER THIRTY-FIVE

He made love to her in the passenger seat of his Lotus, in the Greyhound parking lot at Union station. She was glad she'd worn a dress for easy access, as she raised and lowered her body onto his in the cramped space. She was surprised they fit so well. She was sure they were being watched, but Jake reminded her several times that his windows were tinted, so they could only see out and passersby could only guess what was happening with the car frequently shaking. Jake had turned up hip hop music to hopefully fool them into thinking the car was merely bouncing with the bass.

As she orgasmed, Emma's scream echoed through the alley way behind the station, and at that point she realized the music was not going to cover up her excitement to be with him.

The morning had gone reasonably well. She'd purposefully stayed in bed as Lola got ready for work, but Lola had been nice enough to wish her a safe journey before she left. Clearly, she'd had some time to think about the fit she'd pitched the night before. Emma had walked out of their room to see

Kier on a ladder trying to hang the drapes, and had to admit that they didn't dissuade from the view at all. In fact, they made the apartment look somewhat larger even though they'd first appeared heavy. Kier had an eye for design, and Emma told her as much. Kier had just looked at her sadly and thanked her.

But here she was, now in Portland with her love, and she couldn't be more excited to be away from the Seattle stress. The view as the greyhound arrived over the I-5 bridge was breathtaking, and it was like walking into a new world.

As she moved off of Jake's body and he shifted over, she sat curled up in the passenger seat and rubbed the sides of her thighs, as though attempting to keep the orgasm in them as long as possible, like rubbing a lotion into one's body. Jake took care of the aftermath, hiding the used condom in an old coffee cup. He fired up the engine. As they exited the parking lot, a homeless man raised an empty cup with a "cheers," which made Emma blush and giggle.

"So, what's your news," she asked as they turned onto North Broadway.

"Two things, actually. One, the business is booming! We had a venture capitalist buy in for a million dollars even before the Kickstarter launches!"

"That's amazing!" Emma put a hand on his knee but couldn't take her eyes away from the Portland scenery. All the people were smiling, for the most part. It was so different from the famed 'Seattle Freeze.'

"Second, I think I found a place!"

"You're kidding." Emma was happy for him, but also a bit concerned. If he'd found a tiny condo that would suit Jennifer and himself, then it meant he was probably going to be fine without her there.

"Nope, it's perfect," he continued, "Right near work, great layout, comes with a lot of the furnishings and appliances in place, has a nice big yard for Jennifer to go mouse hunting. It's great."

"It's a house, then? You decided against the condos in the Pearl district?"

"Yeah. The owner wants to close fast, so I can move in within a few weeks, I think."

"I see." She didn't want to seem bugged by his moving on with his life, so she perked up. "That's fantastic. So where are we going now?"

"You and I have a date with Voodoo doughnuts, remember?"

#

The line at Portland's famous doughnut shop wasn't very long at all, and within a short time they were enjoying their coffee and chocolate glazed in Jake's car, heading East across the Burnside bridge.

"What do you think?" She asked him.

He chewed the doughnut slowly and nursed his coffee. "It's not... amazing."

"You go for the clientele and the experience, not the food."

He raised an eyebrow. "I'm glad we didn't line up on Saturday."

She giggled, and watched the downtown area disappear in her rearview mirror. "So, are we heading to your office?"

"Actually, I'm having the realtor meet us at the house I'm interested in. I want your opinion."

"Why does my opinion matter? If you like it, buy it." She shrugged out the car window.

"It matters, because I expect you to have sex with me in it."

Emma blushed. "You're ridiculous. As proven by this morning at the greyhound station, I'd have sex with you anywhere."

"Which is totally awesome, and for that reason I don't want to lose you because of a house, you see?" He laughed as he turned onto 12th Street.

The area looked familiar to Emma, and she figured it was because they'd been there the previous weekend. Or perhaps she'd been here when she was younger, she couldn't quite put her finger on it. As Jake pointed toward the For Sale sign, memories came flooding back to Emma and she gasped.

"What? You hate it already?" Jake parked the car in front of the house and waved at Carla, his realtor.

"No." Emma got out of her car and stared agog at the house. Kier's house. Brent and Kier and Tor's house. She'd been here many times with Lola.

"It's a 1990s two-story Craftsman," smiled Carla, obviously mistaking Emma's reaction for amazement.

Jake shook the woman's hand. "Emma, you remember Carla. She's a friend of my mom's."

"Nice to see you again," Carla smiled, "Jake talks about you all the time."

Emma couldn't take her eyes from the house. "It's... for sale?"

"Wonderful, isn't it? The previous owners took great care of it, it's in great shape."

"Of course they did. Of course it is," was all Emma could muster. She didn't know whether to stay or flee. "Why are they selling?" A stupid question, she knew, because she already knew why Brent was selling. But she wondered what the realtors were telling each other.

"The couple is divorcing, unfortunately."

Did Kier know they were divorcing? If Jake knew the previous owner was a cheating bastard, would he be so keen to jump on this deal? She wondered. She watched Carla and Jake walk up the sidewalk toward the front door, but had trouble moving herself.

Jake ran back to grab her hand. "Come on! I'd really like you to see the inside. They have a nice layout upstairs with a--"

"Theater room, I know. And built-in surround."

Jake stared at her, puzzled, but Carla was holding the door open for them, so he led her up the front walkway.

It had been years since she'd been here, but most of the outside was the same. Well-manicured bushes had gone slightly astray in the past two weeks, but still sang of Kier's tender gardening skills. Emma wondered if Kier was bugging out without flowers to plant in Seattle. She made a note to purchase some greenery for the apartment when she returned.

Inside, the house was immaculate. The furnishings were expensive, thanks to Brent being quite high up in the shipping industry, and Kier having an eye for interior design. They'd never been ones for knickknacks and personal photos, so decluttering for a sale must have been easy for Brent.

"If you'll come this way to the kitchen, I'll show you the stunning--"

"Granite countertops and stainless-steel appliances," Emma finished the sentence. Again, she got looks, but Jake must have shrugged it off to being a normal occurrence in an up-to-date house.

Emma didn't ogle the kitchen as Carla and Jake did, instead she walked straight to the fridge to see what was inside. Kier always had amazing food. Had it gone stale in her absence?

Carla was taken aback. "The appliances are included, although normally it's not something people look inside."

Jake raised an eyebrow but was beginning to sense that something was amiss.

"Can I see the office?" Emma hurried.

"You don't want to see the rest of the downstairs?" Carla was surprised.

"No, just the office."

"Upstairs is technically three bedrooms, but one *is* being used as an office, and--"

Before Carla could finish the thought, Emma rounded the corner from the kitchen and bounded up the staircase. She knew the office well. It was where Lola and she had stayed when they'd last visited years ago. Tor's room was next to it. He was only a young boy when she'd been there last. She wondered if his room was still decorated in Spider Man, and stole a glance into it. Nope, he'd updated it in his teens to celebrating the University of Portland Pilots, where he now went to school. He was an adult now, she told herself. She wondered if he knew the house was for sale.

She raced to the master bedroom, firmly off limits when she and Lola were girls. This was Kier and Brent's private space, and they'd never been allowed to see beyond a glimpse inside. As she suspected, it was wonderfully decorated with a large seating area and its own master ensuite bathroom, complete with a jacuzzi tub.

Stunning, she thought, *and exactly what I expected Kier would live in.*

She felt like a college kid again, banished to the smaller second-floor bathroom and forced to share it with a six year-old who couldn't quite pee straight yet.

Back in the master bedroom, she ogled the fine linens and minimalist decor on the nightstand. She couldn't quite tell which side had been Brent's and which was Kier's, a thought that made her sad, wondering how long he'd been checked out of their relationship. She made a note to talk more to Kier when she returned. She hadn't paid much attention to her split at all, she'd been so caught up in her new relationship and lack of her own bedroom. Kier was hurting far worse than Emma could ever imagine.

She went to the dresser near the walk-in closet and opened a few drawers, until she spotted them -- framed photographs of their family. The kind everyone has in their room but that must be tucked away when selling a house, so that the prospective buyers can 'see themselves in it', instead.

A photo of Tor at his high school graduation was framed in ornate gold, obviously a cherished piece. But it was a smaller photo near the bottom of the drawer which stood out at Emma. The sisters and herself in the backyard at a barbeque. Brent had taken the picture just as rain had begun to fall, and the girls were squealing and half bent over. Kier looked protective of her and Lola, like a mother, even though they were nineteen or twenty or so at that time.

Jake and Carla walked into the room and caught her with the photo over the open drawers. "What are you doing?" Carla's disapproval was palpable. House hunters are not supposed to go into people's personal belongings at all, and here Emma was with several items in her hand.

"Wait," Jake held Carla back and walked over to Emma, taking the photo from her and gazing at it. At his recognition of her younger self, first he smiled. Then he frowned. "I honestly had no idea," he assured Emma.

"How could you know?" She shrugged. She wasn't hurt or overwhelmed or even puzzled at him possibly buying the house. She actually found herself completely indifferent. She only hoped that Kier was okay. A rough estimate of Oregon's divorce rules left her more confused as ever. Was the house only in Brent's name? Did she get a cut of it? After at least 20 years in the place, they must own a significant portion, if not the whole thing outright.

Jake waved the picture at Carla trying to assure her that Emma wasn't crazy. "She knows these people."

"The wife is in my bedroom right now," Emma added. "I'm sorry I didn't mention it before. I wanted to be absolutely sure."

"So you're not interested, then?" Carla seemed upset and skulked back out of the bedroom.

"Wait." Jake ran after her, but looked back at Emma as if to say, "I don't know, *am* I interested?"

Emma shrugged again. He was his own man; he could buy whatever house he wanted. She followed them both downstairs and out the front door.

Carla stopped by the garden. "It's not like this is the first time this has ever happened. In fact it happens a lot, you know. The housing market is pretty good right now. If you're interested, Jake--" She emphasized his name and glared at Emma as if to say *stay out of this, woman.* "--You should put an offer in."

Jake looked at Emma, then back to Carla, in a typical clueless and helpless male way. It made Emma laugh.

He said, "Let me think about it and I'll call you tonight, Carla. Thanks for coming out."

"I'll tell your mother you say hi." Carla stole another angry glance at Emma and stomped back to her Mercedes. Emma curled a lip. *With a car like that, I'm sure you do just fine with or without his commission, lady.* As Jake turned back toward her, she smiled innocently. Women's head games are not something he wanted to mess with.

"Truth be told, it is a little more than I wanted to spend, anyway," Jake offered. "I just thought it would be a great place to--"

"Jake, I don't want you to turn down a great deal. Not for this. People move all the time." Emma stole a glance at her phone, wondering if she should call Kier. Then she realized it would be ridiculously rude to call the woman on the phone and tell her the ex was selling the house and *oh, hey, can my boyfriend buy it?*

As if he read her mind, Jake said, "You want to go back to Seattle again, don't you?"

"I should talk to her in person," Emma said. "And judging by the rushed tone of Carla, we should get on this purchase soon."

"Don't pay attention to her, she's a realtor. They always say things like 'there's a lot of interest' and 'grab it now before it flies off the market.'"

Emma laughed and punched Jake in the arm, playfully. "Look at you learning how realtors work!"

Jake laughed. "Come on, let's grab lunch and a hotel room, I'll bring you back to the bus station tomorrow morning. For today, you're all mine."

"Hotel room first, then lunch," Emma giggled, and squeezed his firm buttcheek.

CHAPTER THIRTY-SIX

I t was just as well that Emma left after only a
night with Jake. They'd spent all afternoon deep in each other's
embrace, and as a result he'd missed a big meeting at work.

"Thankfully, they're my friends. They'd miss a meeting
for sex, too," he'd said as he helped Emma pack her bag
Thursday morning.

Still, she felt bad. She didn't want to be the reason his
work fell under the radar. As of that moment, he was the only
one of them still employed. She said as much as he dropped her
off at the bus station.

"When will I see you again?" He asked as he pulled into
the same parking spot he'd picked her up in the day before, in
more ways than one. Her belly did a flip as he ran his hand up
her leg, but the bus was coming soon. She wondered if they'd
have time for a quickie.

She didn't have time to guess. He reached over the
console in the Lotus and ran a hand up under her skirt and
started kissing her neck.

"I don't know about this." She ran her hand through his hair and kissed him back. "I have to go if I'm going to catch my bus."

Jake groaned and removed his hand from her body. As his fingers departed, she groaned too. It would be a bitter and empty bus trip, she knew.

"If I don't go now, you'll get no work done. They need you."

Jake nodded and opened his car door. He walked around to her door and helped her out, then went to the trunk to get her bag. She paused at the trunk and kissed him hard, rubbing her body against his. She could feel his muscles ache under her touch, and against her heat she could feel him harden despite the crisp Portland air.

"Stop teasing me, woman, or I'll push you into this trunk and never let you go," he said between heated kisses.

"*You'll* push *me* in? I was thinking of pushing you in and swiping this sweet ride with you as my hostage. I wonder how far I'd get."

"I'd go anywhere with you," he said, and shut the trunk behind them. "But today, you go to Seattle." He handed her the suitcase and offered to walk her into the bus station.

She shook her head. "Go, save your parking money. We'll need the extra time on the meter when I get back."

He raised an eyebrow and smiled. "So you'll come back, then. Good, it's decided."

"Was there ever any question?" Now it was her turn to be puzzled.

"No, it's just that every time you come here you leave after a day. I'm beginning to think the idea of Portland scares you off."

"I grew up here, remember?" She punched him in the arm and left his embrace, pulling her suitcase handle up so that it would roll on the pavement. "I love Portland."

"Well I love you," he winked at her and rounded the car to his door.

That was the first time she'd ever heard those words out loud from a man. As he got in his car and closed the door, she said "I love you too."

#

She'd been home for a few hours, but there was still no sign of Kier and Lola. Her texts were going ignored, too. Finally, Emma decided to eat leftovers and chill out in front of a repeat of *Love, Actually.*

'Tis the season, she smiled to herself. With a beer, a romantic comedy and a cozy blanket in her possession, she soon fell asleep on Hetty's old couch.

Emma didn't know how long she'd been asleep when she heard the door open. Judging by the giggles and masculine chortle, someone had a man over. She propped her body up to peer over the back of the sofa, as Lola stumbled into the living room with someone in a suit, and Kier following along behind them.

"Emma!" Lola beamed, drunkenly half-yelling. "You're here! Look what I brought home!"

"Hi. I'm Dale." The man stretched out a hand to introduce himself. His clean crisp suit was pressed just at the right angle so as to make his arms seem longer, but Emma still had to adjust herself to reach out and shake it. She held the blanket tight over her pajamas.

Kier closed the front door and walked in behind them. Emma shot her a look trying to ask *is Lola okay?* Kier seemed to read the tone correctly and shrugged. She went to her room, removing her coat.

"You'll never guess what he does!" Lola giggled.

"Corporate Lawyer?"

Dale's jaw dropped. "Wow, how'd you guess?! That's exactly what I do!"

"Isn't it sexy? Come on, Le Juris Docteuuurr" Lola slurred her words and pushed him toward the bedroom. "You're welcome to squeeze into bed with us if you want, Emmammmemma."

Dale face lit up in a lascivious grin, as Lola began unbuttoning her shirt. She pushed him into the room.

"Thanks, but no thanks. I'm good out here."

"Oh, that's right," drawled Lola. "She has a boyfriend." She sang this last word like a high school mean girl.

Emma laughed; Dale seemed disappointed.

As if.

The lack of size in the apartment was most apparent when sex was happening. In the past, one girl would leave while the other was getting it on, or they'd just stay in their bedroom with the door closed. But since Emma didn't really have a bedroom at the moment, she was stuck on the couch right outside Lola's room, listening to her giggle and moan as Corporate Lawyer Dale had his way with her.

It was both arousing and slightly embarrassing to listen to them pant like animals behind the closed door.

Kier came out of her room in more comfortable jeans and a t-shirt, and sighed. "I am not built for clubbing," she said.

The groaning grew louder. "Doesn't this bother you?" asked Emma. "She's your baby sister."

"She's an adult, she can screw who she wants."

"But the sound of it? Yikes." Emma threw the blanket off herself and stomped to the kitchen with her dishes.

Kier watched her furiously wash a dish, smiling. "I can't figure out if you're envious or jealous."

Emma paused and dropped the dish and towel in the sink. It clattered against the stainless steel, and a part of her hoped the noise would be enough to shut the two lovers up.

"I don't know what the difference is, Kier. Enlighten me." She rolled her eyes.

Kier picked up the dish again and began washing it. "Envy is coveting something someone else has, in this case you could be envious of Lola for getting laid when you're not--" she gave Emma the once-over, as if trying to assuage whether she'd had sex lately or not. Emma felt a little violated by the look, but kept her mouth closed. "Jealousy is the feeling you get when something is taken away from you."

"Well, that doesn't make any sense," Emma stated. "Nothing has been taken away from me except my bedroom, and you did that first."

"Okay." Kier's voice raised a few notes as if to mock Emma. She turned back to the sink.

The sounds in the bedroom died down to a lull. "Thank goodness he didn't last long," muttered Emma, grabbing the dish towel and helping Kier with dishes.

"Mmm-hmm," Kier said.

What is she getting at, anyway? Am I envious or jealous of who? Lola? Dale? She struggled to figure Kier out, but in the end figured she was just a complete lunatic and that this divorce had sent her too far off her rocker.

The divorce! She'd almost forgotten what she came here for.

She put a hand on Kier's arm to stop her from scrubbing more dishes. "Kier, we need to talk. You should grab a beer."

CHAPTER THIRTY-SEVEN

They sat down on the sofa together, two beers open and both with a leg tucked up under themselves. Emma didn't beat around the bush. "So, you know I'm seeing that guy."

Kier laughed. "I like the way you say that, like you're teenagers again. Yes, Jake."

"He's house hunting in Portland. That's what I was visiting him for, to help."

"Good, he could use your eye for space. People who live in small apartments have a great eye for the practical use of space." Kier smiled widely.

Emma continued. "Yesterday we looked at a house. Your house."

Kier's grin froze, but the smile turned from genuine to fake in a flash, almost imperceptibly so. The corners of her eyes fell and the laugh lines she typically sported on her forty-six-year-old cheeks turned to wrinkles before Emma's eyes. She sat there, seconds passing by, her face aging a thousand years in an instant as thoughts ran through her brain.

Emma didn't know whether to keep watching or run far away, like she'd committed a crime. She looked down at her hands and realized Kier was holding on to them. *Why is she holding* me*? I should be holding her.* Emma attempted to move one finger, but Kier's grasp wouldn't budge. There was no running away even if she'd tried.

"So," Kier's voice broke, raising then lowering an octave. "What did you think?"

Emma looked back at her. The grin was starting to transform back into a real smile. "What did I think about what?"

"The house! What did you guys think about the house. It's in decent shape, right? We never did much to it except a few updates from the 90s, but we kept it in good form. It just got a new roof this past year, in fact." Kier patted Emma's hands and let go, leaving a cold chill in her wake. She reached for her beer and kissed it lightly, barely taking a sip. Her eyes watched Emma for some sort of response.

"It—well--" Emma tried to choose her words, "It looks great. Just like I remembered it, although Tor's room didn't have the big Spider-man decal it once did."

Kier laughed and patted her knee, leaning further back into the couch. "That Spiderman sticker has been gone for several years. I can't believe you haven't been back in that time."

"I think I have, it's just that we haven't stayed there for a while."

"Ah yes, you guys stayed with Mom the last few holidays, right? That's probably my fault. I thought we didn't have space. How silly was that – look at the space all around us!" Kier grabbed the remote and turned on the television, resting on the weather channel. Emma's eyes didn't move from her, she sat affixed on Kier's bizarre demeanor. "Oh! That reminds me, Christmas is coming up soon. I should figure out what Tor needs. Probably money." Kier flipped the channel and landed on an old episode of the Simpsons.

Bart sang "you don't win friends with salad" on the screen, which made Kier laugh again.

What is happening here? Emma was transfixed by the strangeness. She began to open her mouth to ask, "So you knew about this?" but Lola's door opened before she could get out the first word.

The Corporate Lawyer guy tip-toed out of the room quietly and held up a finger to his lips. If he was embarrassed at their sex being heard, he didn't show it at all. *Typical lawyer, unashamed of anything*, Emma thought.

"Tuckered that one out, I think." He winked at Emma. Kier stared at the screen.

Emma rolled her eyes. "The door is over there. You have to jiggle the handle a bit."

"You ladies can jiggle my handle any time," he smiled. "Maybe we could do that threesome next time."

Now it was Kier's turn to roll her eyes, but as they were still facing the television, only Emma saw it. They smiled in unison, and Emma ignored further talk with him. There would be no next time, she knew. That's not how Lola fucking corporate lawyers worked. They were only ever one-nighters for Emma's best friend. As the door closed behind him, Emma found comfort knowing he was gone forever. She no longer felt envy.

Or was it jealousy? I forget the difference.

#

Emma slept curled next to Lola's naked body, her best friend not having woken since her sexcapade. She'd gotten a glass of water and an aspirin and left them on Lola's side of the bed, knowing she still had a full day of work ahead of her when she rose.

Her conversation had ended with Kier shortly after the lawyer had left, nothing more than casual chat about what season of the Simpsons was currently airing, and if they were a Simpsons character, which one would they be?

Kier: Lisa.

Emma: Ned Flanders was her best guess, she didn't really watch the show.

In the morning, Lola woke with a hangover and curled around Emma, moaning. Emma attempted to sleep through it but signaled to the pills at the side of the bed. Lola crawled her way out the door to the shower. The fresh smell of Eggs Benedict wafted through the open bedroom door, and Emma couldn't help but wake up for it.

As though alcohol meant nothing to Lola, she bounced out of the shower a whole different person, fresh as the day was young, and starving for breakfast.

"Good night last night?" Kier quizzed her sister in the slyest of tones, which made Emma laugh and slightly spit out her orange juice.

"Thank you, dear sister, yes. I got what I needed out of that fellow. What was his name again?"

This time it was Kier's turn to laugh, and Emma joined in. Soon all three were laughing hysterically at the previous evening's transgressions, making jokes about Dale's idea of a three-way and how he'd rocked Lola's world. "Well, it wasn't *that* great," teased Lola. "It didn't even last the length of a closing argument!"

Realizing the time, Lola popped up and began collecting dishes.

"I'll do them, babe," Emma said through a mouth full of toast.

"Thanks," Lola dashed to find her bag. "Ladies, tonight? Bingo!"

"Oh, I--" Emma tried to come up with a reason not to.

"--would be delighted!" Kier finished her sentence for her.

Lola grinned and dashed out the door, as Kier shot Emma a look.

When Lola had left, she spoke. "My baby sister needs this."

"She needs Bingo?"

"It's better than lawyers, isn't it? That's her other option, you know."

Emma sighed in agreement. She was done with corporate lawyers, she'd hoped Lola would follow suit soon, too. "Bingo, though. Bingo," she said this with great disdain.

"Hey, it's worked out for you so far."

Emma smiled. Jake was a great bingo prize, she could definitely agree to that. If she never won another full card again in her life, Jake was the full card of a lifetime.

Jake, her mind came back around to the conversation from the night before. "Kier, your house," was all she got out, before Kier tut-tutted her and began stacking dishes in front of Emma. Emma took the cue and collected the dirty dishes from the table, walking them to the sink and running the water.

Obviously, Kier didn't want to talk about it, but what was Jake to do? Truth be told it was a great price in an excellent location, so he'd be a fool not to scoop it up.

As she did the dishes, Kier got ready to go out. "I'm thinking of hitting some local breweries for a better selection in the fridge. Want to join me for a tour or two?"

"Thanks, but no. I'd better text Jake and see how he's doing."

Kier pulled on a jacket and shifted her long blonde locks out of the back of it, waving them behind her. Emma admired her body and style, which didn't seem to age at all with her. As Kier opened the door to leave, she turned and looked at the floor, then back up at Emma, who was still watching her with amazement.

"It was a lovely house to raise a family in," was all she said. And then she drifted out the door.

CHAPTER THIRTY-EIGHT

JO: So what's the verdict? My realtor wants to go ahead with an offer today before they hold an open house.

ES: I don't know. I guess it's your choice, do what you want.

JO: What does that mean? Does that have a hidden meaning? Does that mean no?

ES: No, silly, it means do what your heart tells you.

JO: But you did talk to her, right? She gave her OK?

ES: She didn't really give an answer either way, that's why I'm telling you to do what your heart tells you.

JO: It's a well-kept house in a great location. I can practically walk to work.

ES: I know, it's a great price, too.

JO: So I'm doing it, then. I'm buying a house.

ES: Great.

JO: I feel like there is subtext.

ES: There is no subtext. Great!

JO: I'm going to call Carla. 8D

Jake logged off before she could respond. Emma didn't know what to say, anyway. There wasn't subtext, she was sure, she wanted him to own a good house near his office, and so what if it was her best friend's sister's divorce house? A good deal is a good deal.

Emma paced the living room for a few minutes while she considered the possible repercussions. Jake was his own guy, buying a house that happened to belong to someone she knew. So what? Big deal! What if they were never in a relationship in the first place?

He would have bought the house the first minute he walked into it, right?

No, because he would have fallen for a visually large, tiny apartment, and he would be living in a condo in the Pearl district, like a bachelor.

Truth was, Emma had encouraged him to seek something larger, something with space to work, play, and... *raise a family.*

Her womb ached with longing, and she grabbed a beer to try and quash the thoughts and emotions her hormones caused. "Feminists don't desire children!" She screamed into the bottlecap as she struggled to pop it off on the side of the counter.

"Actually," Kier entered the front door of the apartment, "feminism is about a woman's right to choose whatever she wants, to be equal to her male counterparts. If a man wants to have a baby or not have a baby, nobody bats an eye and he can find someone to do those things with. If he wants to work or stay home, he has the right to choose to work or stay home. Feminism seeks out those equal life choices."

Emma was embarrassed at her ridiculous outcry, and also slightly alarmed by Kier's arrival home. She hadn't been gone long enough to tour much of anything.

"Did you just *Well, Actually* me Kier? Are you saying you're a feminist, then? You've never worked a day in your life."

Kier gave her a look as though she were completely clueless and needed a pat on the head. "I chose to stay home with my son, and I *did* work, I volunteered in the school, I helped Brent develop his business--" at this, her face fell ever so slightly, but Emma could tell it was a mark of bitterness rather than sadness. "It may not have gotten me very far, but I chose it because it's what worked best for my family. But I rally right alongside any woman in the world who demands equal pay in the workforce, or the right to control her own body. That's what feminism is."

"Oh."

"If your body is telling you it desires children--" Kier's eyes quickly darted to Emma's womb, which flashed with an ache of emptiness again, then back up to her eyes. "--Then you need to listen and figure out what that means for you."

Emma felt uncomfortable. She sipped her drink and moved past Kier to sit on the sofa and flip through designer magazines. Her eyes couldn't follow the page, though. As Kier began to remove her jacket, Emma's eyes roamed any direction they could, squaring in on the new velour curtains Kier'd had delivered barely a day before.

"Where'd the curtains come from, Kier?"

Her new roommate paced from the closet to the kitchen, and she began to butter a piece of bread. "The house, I told you. A friend sent them. I thought they'd be perfect for your windows."

"Who sent them?"

"A friend," Kier repeated herself innocently, and took a bite of her plain bread with butter.

"A friend who knew your house was going on the market this week? Before you yourself even found out?"

Kier was silent for a minute, Emma surmised that she was weighing how much she should say. Kier had always seen herself as the more knowledgeable, older and wiser sister, sharing life lessons--or just basic English lessons in the case of the envy/jealous and feminism soliloquies-- with Emma and Lola. Emma purposefully remained silent so that Kier could process that maybe in this case Emma had figured something out that Kier didn't want her to know.

Finally, Kier spoke. "He sent them to me because he knew they were my favorite, I suppose. I guessed that he was going to list the house, and that he didn't want a buyer asking for them in the deal." She sat down on the couch beside Emma and stared at the curtains, their rich red velvet barely swaying in her breeze. "He was and is a really wonderful man, you know. He just made a stupid mistake."

"He cheated on you! He left you for a woman barely half your age!"

"It was a midlife crisis."

"That doesn't matter, Kier! He's selling the house you raised his son in! He's giving all of this up--" Unable to show off Kier's house, she waved at Kier and the curtains-- "for a hotsy totsy in high heels!"

Kier's face turned to a smile, as Emma's indignancy waned. Together, they laughed out loud at the ridiculousness of Emma's statement.

Kier said, "Hotsy-totsy? You sounded just like Grandma Hetty there."

"Channeling the room, I guess," Emma blushed. In that moment she realized that she had no idea what twenty years of marriage looked like or felt like, never having had a relationship last more than a few months. Kier must have loved him and trusted him, to help him succeed the way he had, to stand nobly and innocently by, raising their only son, for the man she adored.

Emma felt like a fool. "I'm sorry."

"It's okay," Kier nodded, but Emma could see that it really was not. "It's not like I don't think about this every day. When you told me the house was listed for sale, I think I finally got it. That's why I came home early. I began walking to my car and just thinking, and I realized this is it. He won't be back, maybe he never intended to be back. But just because he used me for twenty years doesn't mean he was a bad human, he was just a failure as a husband. I still like him, and I'm thankful that he thought to save my favorite curtains from being sold, but I'm also angry. Like, really really angry."

Emma sat still. It looked as though Kier was going to continue a thought. To spur her on, she quietly whispered, "Angry about the curtains?"

"No! I'm angry that he didn't remember that my favorite permanent fixture is the chandelier in the dining room! God damn it, it's a Chihuly-style glass sculpture! Fuck these curtains!"

Emma's shock at hearing Kier use a swear word was evident, but turned almost instantly to laughter. Then Kier's anger did, too. They laughed into their bread and beer, and spent the rest of the afternoon watching mindless television and muttering "Fuck these newscasters!" and "Fuck these beers!"

CHAPTER THIRTY-NINE

Lola met them at the early Bingo game. Kier and Emma had already claimed their seats beside Lillian and Mabel, and as Lola approached the table, the four women were chortling over Mabel's new penis-shaped Bingo dabber. It was unintentional, Mabel said, but with the extra round lid and textured base, it made it easier for her old hands to hold and was almost identical to a circumcised penis. It had been Kier who first noticed it.

"What are we laughing at, ladies?" Lola bent down over Kier and hugged her around the shoulders, her crisp work suit restricting her movement. She undid the jacket and pulled it off, causing a commotion in the local tables as she did so. Her pert breasts jutted out as she pulled the jacket off her arms, and Emma wondered if Lola even knew that whenever she moved, people stared.

"Look at what Mabel bought," Lillian was still giggling. Mabel held the bingo dabber in the air and motioned it up and down like she was giving it a hand job. The elder ladies chortled some more.

"Penis dabber, awesome! I bet that brings back a lot of memories, right Em?" Lola rounded the table and put a hand on Emma's shoulder as she squeezed into a seat between her and Mabel.

Emma blushed, reminded of the wild night with Jake only a week before. She'd forgotten that she'd shared the entire events, down to the last detail, with her best friend.

"Ooooh," Lillian and Mabel laughed in unison and winked, and even though she didn't know what they were talking about, Kier laughed, too.

The game began slowly, as Mary introduced numbers in her nervous voice. The mood in the Bingo parlor had definitely been quieter since Jake's departure, but everyone was still giddy with excitement as their cards began to fill up. Kier and Mabel both got down to an almost full card, Kier waiting for B-11 and Mabel waiting on the elusive N-41. As the tension mounted, they began a friendly rivalry yelling "mine is next, I can feel it!" and "if I win this, I'm not sharing!" Unfortunately, the final number was G-55, and lady at the table across from them turned to a person beside her and screamed, "Look, Mama! They got my age and your number! BINGO!"

Kier and Mabel frowned into their papers, looking around for any card they'd missed with a G-55 on it, but coming up empty. At this point Kier offered to buy Mabel a soda, and frustratedly left the table before the intermission began.

Emma was glad Lola was back to her regular self, happily stamping numbers and laughing with the older women. The frustration of earlier in the week seemed to have disappeared completely, Lola at several times giving Emma friendly jabs in the arm over humorous jokes, and making fun of the caller along with her. As they playfully teased Mabel about her penis dabber, the tension of the entire few weeks completely disappeared.

"Hey stranger."

"Hey yourself, how's Portland?"

"Kinda meh right now, trying to figure some things out." Jake's voice on the phone was hard to read, but Emma surmised that things weren't going as well as he'd indicated.

"Wanna talk about it?"

"Are you alone?"

"Why? Are you meh because you're lacking phone sex?" Emma giggled into the phone and Kier looked up from where she was sitting under the window. She faked a look of haughty derision, but she winked.

"Well, yes, that too. But I also wanted to talk about the house."

"Oh." She looked at Kier and wondered how to get out of the room. "Well, I'm just going down to collect my laundry, so we can do it there." She winked at Kier as she donned her shoes and grabbed her empty laundry basket, quickly leaving the apartment with the phone tucked under her chin. Once she was safely halfway down the stairs, she said, "Okay, what's up?"

"The deal fell through. There are two better offers on the table, with a bigger down payment than I have."

Emma knew they hadn't really talked about finances beyond the basics she knew from his paperwork at Microsoft, but she felt like he was letting her into that safe space with his realty talk. "What happened to your severance? Your stocks?"

"I spent them all on this company."

"Wait!" She tripped on the last step and stumbled into the laundry room. "*You're* the venture capitalist they found?"

"It's a great product, and we've already lined up a Chinese manufacturer, but until it goes into production I'm not going to get my money back."

"So, how much do you have left for a down payment?" Emma began to empty out the dryer, trying to fold her clothes with the phone under her ear. Her mind began to race, and she suddenly felt like this house was the key to something. He needed to get this house.

"Like eighty grand, which would be fine for a small condo in Portland, but I guess this area is hot, and this is a great house."

"It *is* a great house. It has amazing features and--" Emma suddenly remembered the light fixture Kier wanted. "You need to get this house."

"What happened to 'maybe I shouldn't buy Kier's house.'"

"That was before I realized what was at stake. It's the light fixture."

Jake was puzzled. "The one in the dining room?"

"It's the only thing Kier wants out of that house. I was hoping you'd get it so she could take it out of the deal. The way things are now, Brent has all the power to sign those documents, since he's the only homeowner. He doesn't know that the fixture is what Kier wants."

"Could we find him and tell him?"

"Kier doesn't know where he's living. And it would be weird for you, a total stranger, to go find him at work and tell him not to sell a light fixture, wouldn't it?"

"Yeah, I guess that *would* be weird." Jake's voice was soft, as though he were thinking hard about what to do. "But I can't make an offer with money I don't have. Maybe she'll just have to let it go."

"I'll buy the house." Emma shocked even herself when she said it.

"I--what?" Jake was equally shocked. "No, that's--"

"Completely logical? I'm the only one with money in this scenario. My severance was huge and because I barely pay rent here, I have a ton of money."

"Like a sugar Momma? I feel kind of strange letting you buy a house for me."

"Consider me a venture capitalist in your success, I guess. Get on the phone with Carla. We'll do an all-cash offer."

"Emma, I can't--"

"What? You can't let me buy real estate? I'm not some bride with a dowry. I can rent that house out to someone else, you know. You don't have to be the proud misogynist man in this relationship, you know."

"I—" Jake fell silent on the phone, as though running numbers through his head. "Okay, I'll call Carla." Then he added, "--and Emma?"

"Yes?" Emma had never felt more confident in a decision in her life. She was excited to be a landlord, even if it was in Portland. At least it was *sort of* like having a job.

"Move in with me."

"What?"

"Let's live together. Here, in *your* house."

"I--" Emma was floored. "I'll have to think about that, Jake."

"Of course, I understand. I'll talk to you soon." His voice sounded slightly crushed, but she didn't like being put on the spot either.

"Okay. Hey Jake?"

"Yeah."

"I love you."

"You're buying me a house. I guess you must," he laughed, and hung up the phone.

CHAPTER FORTY

Emma collected the rest of the laundry, threw her phone down on it, and walked upstairs.

"I'd be a homeowner? Why shouldn't I be a homeowner?" She repeated the questions out loud to herself several times, just to work it through her brain. She was nearing thirty-six, why shouldn't she own a home by now?

Except that the home she was buying was in the wrong city, nowhere near where her life was.

She used her back to open the door into the apartment and failed to notice Lola opening the door behind her, an act which made her stumble and trip into Lola's arms.

Lola stammered, "Woah, lady!"

"Oh, Lola hey, sorry I didn't see you," Emma muttered as she straightened herself.

"I heard you coming up the stairs, you were talking to yourself pretty loud there, babe." Lola assisted by taking the laundry basket and sorting through it.

Emma's phone began to ring, and Lola looked down at it. "Portland area code is calling you, I wonder who that could be?" She said with snark and handed the phone to Emma.

"Hello?"

"Emma, it's Carla, Jacob Ono's realtor? We met--"

"Oh, hi Carla, I'm glad you called!"

Lola looked back over her shoulder with a puzzled expression. She mouthed the word "Carla?" but continued taking the clothes to the bedroom.

Emma went into the kitchen, smiling briefly at Kier on the sofa, but trying to hold the phone down where neither Kier nor Lola could hear her. With the laundry now done, she had no more excuses to leave the apartment.

Carla got down to brass tacks and began talking. "So Jacob explained your plan, and I think we should go through with a full price, cash offer. I need to know that you're on board with that and can get the money soon if that's how we're going to write this up."

"Hmm-mmm, yup. I'm on board." Emma rattled around in the sink. Kier looked up from the couch and Lola came back out of the bedroom to sit beside her.

"When do you think you'd have the money by, is it available now?"

"Um, I'd need about a week to pull it out, I think."

Lola's eyebrow raised again.

"A week to get it out of the bank? Okay. Is there anything you'd like me to write up in this offer? Do you need the appliances? That's a fairly standard request."

"Uh, yes. That sounds good."

"What else?"

Emma had to get Kier's light fixture in the deal but do so without attracting the attention of the two girls on the sofa. She thought quickly, but couldn't come up with anything to say. "Light fixture."

Kier raised an eyebrow, but went back to her magazine.

Carla was puzzled "light fixture? Which one?"

Emma shoved her face in the fridge. "Dining." She clanked a beer bottle against another one and pulled it back out again. Lola was giving her an odd look, but Kier hadn't heard. Emma waved the beer bottle at Lola to ask if she'd like one. Lola nodded and smiled and returned to the television. Emma wished the sound was on so she could drown the phone call out.

"Ah yes, that fancy one. Okay, I'll write that up. So, we'll do a full cash offer, no closing cost requests, contingent on inspection?"

"Contingent on inspection?" Emma wasn't sure what those words meant. She'd never bought a house before. Kier closed her magazine and looked up at her, obviously recognizing what she was saying now. Emma turned around and grabbed the second beer.

"It means we'll have an inspector in after the papers are signed, just to make sure the house doesn't have any problems with electrical or foundation and stuff like that."

"Okay, that sounds good." Emma was out of things to do in the kitchen. She hoped the conversation was coming to an end soon.

"So what will happen next is I'll email you some electronic documents that you have to physically sign and scan back to me. After that we can set up a digital signature form that will do it all electronically from you in Seattle to me here in Portland. Does that sound good?"

"Yes."

"I just need your email address."

Emma tried not to look suspicious. She nonchalantly handed a beer to Lola and, upon getting Kier's attention asked her if she'd like one, too. Kier nodded but furrowed her brow in curiosity, as Emma read off her email address.

"Great, please sign that immediately and get it to me by tonight if you can. They have an open house tomorrow and I want to have this in their hands with a 24-hour turnaround before that house gets too many looks. Sound good?"

Emma had no idea what her realtor was saying, so she just grunted her assent and hung up the phone. Now it sounded like she needed a computer, printer and scanner immediately.

"Lola, can I use your computer?" She sat at the small secretary desk near the window and didn't even wait for a response before logging in. Lola shrugged.

The email was sitting there once she got signed in. She sent it to the printer as Kier sat and watched the machine whir to life. She also dusted off the photocopier and scanner.

Kier watched the whole thing with her chin tilted. "Whatcha doin' over there, Em?"

"Not much, Kiki." She hoped the nickname return would shut Kier up. The printer buzzed out the form, and she grabbed a pen and signed it, throwing it back on the scanner before Kier or Lola could get a look at what it was.

"Whatcha signing?" Now it was Lola's turn to slur her words as she quizzed her roommate.

"Just some papers."

"Job offer?"

"It's not important. What's on TV?" She attempted to stare at the TV as the scanner program ran. Kier watched the image come to life on the computer screen, and Emma tried to block it with her body.

"You're being really evasive," Kier stated.

"She isn't, isn't she?" Lola laughed and rose from the sofa. She walked to the scanner as the machine slowed down, and grabbed the paper off of it.

"Hey," Emma tried to grab it from her hands, but let her keep it. It was only a signature confirmation, it wasn't like they could get that much out of her with it.

"Well, I don't know what this is" Lola waved it around. "It's just a sheet of paper with her name scrawled on it."

Kier stood from the couch. Emma loaded the email again and sent the scanned image off to Carla, while the two other women stared down at the sheet of paper. Kier shrugged. "It's just a box that says, "Sign here?" what are you signing for?"

"Just a signature document. It's nothing."

"It's something," Lola said, but tossed the paper back on top of the printer. "You're hiding something."

"I'm hiding the fact that you're driving me crazy!" Emma closed the computer before they could read her emails over her shoulder.

The two women moved back to the couch and sat down, eyeing Emma closely. Emma's phone beeped in her pocket, and she saw a text from Carla telling her a confidential document would soon be emailed to her that she could sign online.

She closed her phone and decided to wait out the time by being friendly to the women, then she'd escape into the bedroom and do the digital business on her phone, alone.

CHAPTER FORTY-ONE

I know what it was," Kier whispered to Emma as Lola left for the bathroom. The Bingo parlor was beginning to fill with the usual crowd, though Lillian and Mabel had yet to show up.

"I don't know what you're talking about," Emma fidgeted in her bag for her daubers, finally settling her hand on her wallet and wanting to escape to the soda bar and get away from this conversation. She didn't want to let any more information out until she had to.

She'd emailed the digital form back right away, and Carla had said the homeowner, as in Kier's ex-husband Brent, had 24 hours to respond to it. It was entirely possible he would reject it in favor of holding the open house and waiting for more offers to come in. She didn't want to talk about the home purchase with Lola or Kier.

"You're buying real estate," Kier smiled, as Emma began walking toward the soda counter.

"No. I'm just thinking about it," Emma lied.

Kier frowned and sat down in her seat. Shortly, she was accompanied by Lola. Emma hoped they weren't chatting about it at all. Emma ordered three diet cokes, and Aidan fumbled over the machine, counting out the ice cubes one by one. Emma let him this time, as she wanted the conversation to steer away from her and onto something else. Hopefully Kier and Lola would start talking about penis dabbers or something like that.

"How's it going, Aidan?"

Aidan lost count of the cubes in the third glass and restarted it. "Fine, Ma'am."

"Emma."

"Grandma is thinking of making me a bingo caller."

"Oh Aidan, that would be lovely."

"I'm a lousy soda machine guy, what makes you think I could call Bingo numbers?"

"Aw," Emma felt bad for the poor kid. "I'm sure you'd be great at it."

"They don't come out in order, you know." Aidan shuffled the cups until the cubes lined up just right, and Emma wondered what he meant. "The balls. If they came out one at a time, from B-1 to O-75 in order, I'd like it better. This is so random."

"That's what makes it gambling, Aidan!" Emma laughed at him. "If they came out in order, then the only full cards that would win are any with the lowest numbers in each category. What a silly game that would be."

"I would like that game." Aidan began filling the cups, timing when to stop it pouring.

"I bet you would do well at poker. Maybe when you're eighteen you can go down to Vegas and count cards."

"Isn't that illegal?"

"Only if they catch you," Emma snickered and began counting bills out onto the table. She lined them up perfectly, George Washington's head visible on each. Aidan thanked her as he handed her the drinks and collected the money, his mouth moving as he counted them into his own hand. He reached for the till to give her change. "Keep it," she smiled.

As she walked away with the soda cups, she remembered all the times Jake made her spill her drink all over her. Her body missed the shock of his pheromones making her hair stand on end, and the womb-quenching feel of ice cold coke trying to calm her sexual tension back to normal. He wasn't there tonight, and with his business booming and so much money at stake, he probably would never be back.

#

The game began and Lillian and Mabel were nowhere to be seen. As luck would have it for Emma, their absence meant Lola and Kier were preoccupied worrying about where they were and what might be happening, and therefore neither of them mentioned Emma's weird call or paperwork from earlier in the day.

Unfortunately, it dawned on Emma, something terrible could have also happened, and being thankful that their absence was good for her was probably not the best attitude. She attempted to guess possibilities to a very concerned Lola. "Perhaps they went to bed early. Perhaps there was a field trip."

"No," Lola was sure something was wrong. "They never miss Bingo. Never."

"To be fair, we've only been coming here for three weeks," Emma pointed out.

"You don't know them like I do, Emma. You haven't been to many of these, and you didn't visit them that night. Hetty knew them, too. They're here all the time."

Lola's concern grew and grew, as the first half wore on, to the point where she had to leave at intermission.

"Just play my cards, Emma!"

"Lola, you're up to 27 cards! I'm still getting used to my nine!" She panicked. There was no way she could handle this much Bingo all at once.

"I don't care, just do them, I'm leaving." She bailed before Emma could protest further.

Emma gave Kier a pleading appeal. "Please help me, Kier, I don't even know how to play this game."

Kier condemned her, jokingly, "If you'd just focus on the game and not your sexy boy toy and real estate, this wouldn't happen." She grabbed half of Lola's cards, but she also looked seriously overwhelmed.

"Let's just try to do our best, okay?" Emma sighed. "For Lola."

"For Mabel and Lillian!" Kier agreed.

Mary droned the next number, N-34, and the two women furiously attempted to find it on all their cards before the next one popped up, a move that prevented them from talking too deeply about any one subject. This, Emma thought, was another lucky break in her favor. She hoped Mabel and Lillian were just as lucky.

Lola's cards did end up being lucky, but Mabel, unfortunately, was not.

CHAPTER FORTY-TWO

After Bingo, as Emma and Kier entered the senior center, the nurse at the front counter recognized Kier and waved her back toward Mabel's room. Kier attempted to find her bearings as they weaved through the front halls and into the assisted living spaces. Emma passed a disheveled and bent man in a wheelchair. Another man, who looked to be the man's much younger son, tended to his needs. She was grateful Lola had befriended Hetty and these two elderly women.

Who will attend to us when we're old and greying, Lola?

Kier looked in on a door, not remembering if it was Mabel's room or not, and Emma watched her face alight at seeing her sister. Then she bolted into the space. Emma rounded the corner and saw something she never wanted to see again - Mabel's body, blue and cold, lying on the hospital bed. Lillian was holding one hand and Lola the other. A nurse was fiddling with machines.

Emma gasped and remained in the doorway. Kier put a hand on her sister's shoulder and was quiet with her.

They remained in those positions for several minutes, Emma not quite knowing whether to enter the room further or run away and hide. She'd never seen a body before. She'd never known someone who died except for Hetty, and she'd only come down for the funeral and reading of the will.

Finally, Lillian spoke. "She was really grateful to have met you all, and to reconnect with Hetty through you."

Kier perked up, "I just remembered something." She fished into her pocket and removed a thousand dollars, cash. Emma had almost forgotten they'd managed to win the grand money prize.

"Lola, we won this with your cards."

Lola took it and handed it straight to Lillian. "It isn't much, but I want to help with expenses."

"Oh honey, there won't be many expenses. Mabel didn't have any family but me."

"Well, whatever you need for burial, cremation, whatever," Lola said. "Please, take it. It's the least we could do." The sorrow on Lola's face was clear. It was like losing Hetty all over again.

Kier kept a hand on her shoulder, and Emma tried a few times to approach her for a hug but was scared of the body. Scared of what, she wasn't sure. She just knew she wasn't comfortable and didn't know how to make a proper exit.

As if she sensed what was happening in Emma's head, the nurse came around the table and put a hand on her arm. "Would you like me to show you the nurse's station, miss?"

"Oh yes, please." Emma followed her out of the room like a toddler following a ball.

When they were out of earshot, the nurse said, "I could tell you were nervous in there."

"I've never been in a place like this before."

"Assisted living home," the nurse asked. "Never?"

"Never."

She watched a young boy fly a plane down the hallway. "Grandma, grandma, look at me!" he ran past a happy woman sitting on a bench with another, younger woman Emma surmised was the boy's mother.

"What happens next?" Emma wondered out loud.

"Miss Lillian will have to make decisions for Mabel's body."

"Why Lillian? Isn't she just the roommate?"

"No, silly, she's Mabel's girlfriend. She has full power of attorney in this state, thank goodness!"

"Oh wow, I never knew that."

"They started dating after your younger friend's grandma died."

"Hetty? Was Hetty involved with them?"

"Hetty and Mabel were quite an item, and Lillian bided her time until Hetty was gone."

"Wow, that's fascinating. I always thought Hetty got on with younger men. Does Lola know her Grandma was gay?"

"Probably not, but does it matter?"

"No, I guess it doesn't." Emma was fascinated with this news but didn't know what to do with it. Should she tell Lola or no? Did it matter? Maybe it didn't.

Emma waited by the nurse's station, playing with mints and a deck of cards, for a good thirty minutes. She wasn't going to rush the women as they bawled over Mabel's body, so she was happy enough to just play solitaire alone in the waiting area of a senior center. What a strange place to be from four weeks ago, when she'd be picking up another lawyer and rocking his world for those thirty minutes.

She actually liked this better. It was quieter and less risky. She wondered if senior care centers needed HR professionals.

Kier and Lola came out, Lola's face red and bloated with tears, and the three women walked out into the street and headed in the direction of home. They barely spoke to one another, each lost in her own mind, processing what had happened.

When they got home, Emma walked Lola straight to bed, tucked her in, and kissed her lightly on the forehead as she fell fast asleep.

CHAPTER FORTY-THREE

Carla's call came at eight in the morning. Lola, still puffy eyed and miserable, punched Emma a few times until she answered her phone.

Still groggy, Emma hit the answer button and put the phone to her ear.

"Emma, is that you? It's Carla. I have news!"

Emma scrambled out of bed, pulling her robe on and hoping Lola hadn't heard the voice on the other end. Her roommate groaned but kept her eyes shut, and pulled the covers back over her. Emma escaped into the living room and shut the door behind her. Kier was working over the oven, the faint scent of frying turkey bacon wafted into Emma's nose.

"Hmm-mmm" she whispered and attempted to turn down the in-call volume.

"You're a homeowner! Congratulations! He accepted the offer with no corrections, and the owner is desperate to get rid of it, so he's wanting a one-week turnaround time."

"I... that's..." words escaped Emma. She watched Kier flip a piece of toast and wondered if it was okay to gush out loud.

"Isn't it amazing? You'll have to be down here within the next week to sign the paperwork and take the keys, of course."

"Jake can't do that?" she wondered how she could fit another trip to Portland into the next week.

"It's your house, honey, it's not Jake's. He's just your tenant."

Kier looked up at her and waved toward the table, advising Emma to sit and be served breakfast. If she'd noted the phone, she'd ignored it.

"I see. Okay, I guess just let me know when."

"Probably Monday, I'll talk to the homeowner and figure out his plans for moving stuff out."

"Stuff. Stuff." *Kier's stuff!* A million thoughts ran through Emma's head. How would Kier get her stuff? Did it even belong to her? Would Brent try to take it all, or sell it? What about Tor? To Carla, all she said was, "Okay."

"It's a date. Contact your bank today, so we can be sure it's there for next week."

"Money, Monday." Emma's head was pounding with questions. "Okay," was all she said again. Then Carla dropped the call.

Emma stood there with the phone to her ear for five extra seconds, trying to process what had just happened, and what her next steps were. She walked like a zombie to the table and sat down, thinking *what was my next step? What do I do now?* She'd already forgotten.

Kier brought a plate to her, the bacon perfectly browned and eggs sunny side up. *This woman is a master breakfast chef*, thought Emma.

"Money, what? Nobody needs a money conversation on a weekend," Kier noted.

"Money? Money! That's right." Emma remembered what her next move was. She had to juggle money between accounts at the bank. It would have to wait until the next business day, when the banks were open. She punched an alarm into her phone for the next morning.

"What's the rush? Money can't wait for breakfast?" Kier put a hand on her hip and watched Emma set her alarm.

"Sorry, this looks delicious." Emma put the phone in her robe pocket and hoped Kier would stop asking questions she didn't know how to answer.

No such luck. "You're talking about money and stuff, and yesterday you were signing paperwork. What is happening in your life that you're not telling us?" Kier sat down across from her, her own plate of breakfast getting colder as she stared into Emma's face.

"I bought something," was all Emma could get out.

"I know what you bought. I recognized the paper yesterday. Brent has signed many of those digital signature cards. They're mainly used in Real Estate, aren't they?" Kier let that out there and dug into her food.

Emma merely stared into her toast, contemplating what to say next. Soon, her resolve weakened. Kier was too smart for her and there was no backing down from the truth. "I bought a house."

Kier continued to eat her food slowly and carefully, keeping a watchful eye on Emma as though provoking her to dare say more.

Emma's mind raced, but in the end, the truth was going to come out very soon. "I bought *your* house, Kier."

Kier looked into her food and her eyes never strayed as she finished off the last of her breakfast. The clinking of silverware on porcelain was the only brain-crushing sound echoing through the small living space.

Emma could only stare at her food, her stomach had fallen a thousand miles not knowing what would happen next.

"Hey baby girl," Kier's eyes alighted over Emma's shoulder. "How are you doing this morning?"

"You bought my sister's house in Portland?" Lola stood at her bedroom door, incredulous.

Kier got up to make her sister a plate of breakfast.

It seemed like a good idea at the time, Emma thought to herself. *Maybe not so much anymore.*

Lola stomped over to the table and plunked down like a lead weight. She stared at Emma. "When were you going to drop this bombshell on us, Em?"

"I guess when I got the call that my offer was accepted. Which, I suppose I just did."

"What are you planning to do?" Lola's voice was becoming more and more irate, the infuriation growing behind her beautiful green eyes. Emma watched her incredulity turn to fiery rage. Lola cried, "Are you moving there?"

"No, I—Maybe? I don't know."

"Are you moving in with Yoko Ono? Are you going to marry him?! Are you going to have a baby like Kier did and throw your life away?!"

At this, Kier turned and shouted, "Hey--"

Lola held up her hand. "What about *us*, Emma? What about what we have here? What about guys like Dan—"

"—Dale?"

"--Whatever! And you're leaving me right after Mabel's death! You couldn't have waited a day?"

"I didn't say I was leaving," Emma remarked, but then again, she wasn't sure either way. Her womb had been sending signals for weeks now, perhaps this was the universe telling her it was time. As Lola stared into her face, she lowered her voice and lamented, "But maybe it's time I did."

Lola was crushed. "You're just going to give up and go. You're going to leave me and move in with a stranger."

"He's not a stranger, he--" Emma stopped herself. Really, after only a few dates, he was a stranger in comparison to Lola--her best friend of over twenty years. Emma tried to compose her thoughts, to get something logical and sensible out into the air, but none of what she was thinking was logical or sensible at all.

Lola and Kier were silent. Kier served Lola her eggs, but Emma's roommate and best friend just stared into it, sadly.

Emma needed to speak, she knew. It was time. "I love you, Lo. That will never change. But I'm thirty-six years old and I want something more. I've wanted it for a while now."

As Lola frowned and opened her mouth to speak, Emma cut her off. "Before Jake, I even thought about this. I want to have a family, and live in the suburbs, and--"

Lola jabbed at her bacon but said nothing.

Emma wondered what would come of their friendship. Then she noted Kier standing back near the kitchen, and a memory of *whose* house she bought came flashing back to her, too. She'd probably ruined both their lives with this purchase, and she hated herself for it.

Seconds passed, maybe minutes, then Kier spoke. "It was a lovely home," she repeated her thoughts from the previous week. "And it can be again."

Emma got up from the table, not knowing what to say or do. In a flash, she was in Kier's arms, the older Zwanzig hugging her like a mother hugs her baby.

Emma began to cry "I'm so sorry Kier."

"What for? Buying a house? Don't be silly."

Lola stood and leaned from one foot to the other, seemingly troubled.

Emma held out an arm to her and Lola ran into the group hug.

"You're such amazing people," Emma wept. "Lola, you gave me a home when I needed one and you never asked for anything in return. I only hope you come visit me so I can put you up, too. And Kier, you cook for us and you decorated, you raised an amazing son and a powerful asshole husband. You and your sister will get along so well here."

"Oh we will," Kier laughed, "As soon as I replace Hetty's old wrought-iron light fixture with my own."

"You wouldn't dare," Lola teased.

Emma laughed between tears.

Lola said, "Em, you're the best. I wasn't ready for all these changes, but you always have been, and you deserve this.

You'd make an amazing Mom as well. Jake would be lucky to have you raise his children."

Jake. Emma had almost forgotten who had started this whole thing. The three-week whirlwind romance that had caused her to go from being a high-powered corporate executive with a stable and happy life in Seattle, to possibly being an unemployed homeowner in Portland.

"I supposed I'd better call and tell him I'm his landlord," Emma laughed.

EPILOGUE
Nine Months Later

Emma was already waiting on the front porch as Lola pulled into the driveway. Lola appreciated that Emma and Jake had painted their new house, her sister's old house, a completely different color. While Kier's beige exterior had been well-designed and homey, Emma's bright green was just a little bit crazy and a lot more *Portland*.

"Look at you!" Lola gasped as she stepped out of the rental car. "You're positively glowing!"

"Please, I'm a fat cow," Emma laughed and ran into her arms.

"Fetuses are never fat, they're fabulous," Lola laughed. She held her hands out, and after getting the nod from Emma, she felt her belly for kicks. "You'd better name this one after me. I can already tell she's got a curvy butt."

Jake padded out onto the front porch holding a screwdriver. "You're just in time. I need a woman's touch putting the crib together."

"Meaning it didn't come with directions and you need me to figure it out for you?" Lola smirked.

"I just need someone else to blame when it inevitably falls apart," he joked.

Lola rolled her eyes in her quintessential Lola way, which made Emma laugh even more.

"He's all yours, Emma. This is the one you settled for," Lola teased, and she climbed the front stairs to give Jake a hug.

"How's Seattle? How's Kier?" Emma followed them into the house.

"Seattle is Seattle. It grows taller and thicker but it remains dark and damp. Kier has started coming out at night with me more often. She even picked someone up the other night!"

Jake took Lola's bags from her and grinned. "Let me guess, a corporate lawyer?"

"Actually no," Lola said, "a Bingo player!"

"Oh no," Emma and Jake said simultaneously, then smiled at each other.

"I know, right?" Lola joked, "I'm totally going to lose *her* to that wild and sexy lifestyle now, too!"

About the Author

Emmy Tidning lives in a magical fantasy world called the Pacific Northwest, where anything is possible, but no one is real. She has four cats, a dog, a husband, some kids, and a murder of crows who eat her grocery deliveries. Emmy loves Bingo, writes absurd romantic fun, and can be reached through the publisher at info@applieddivination.com

Acknowledgments

This book would not be possible without:

1) Divining Tales, a Paranormal Reader's Group on FB. Although this book is not paranormal, the idea of having sex in a bingo parlor is definitely *out there*.
2) Encouragement from the Romance Writing community, the Cascade Writers organization, and the Speculative Twist Facebook group.
3) The Woot-Tang Clan, who encouraged me to write it in the first place around seven years ago.

Also Published by Applied Divination

Applied Tarot

Applied Runes

Applied Tarot Reversed

Applied Divination Journal

Psychic Word Puzzles

Applied Tasseography

Faye's Fortune

Charlie's Chill

https://emilypaper.com/emmy-tidning.html

Coming soon from Applied Divination

Applied Spells

A Practical Guide to Manifesting Dreams, Blessing Friends, and ~~Cursing Enemies~~ Other Magik

Killer of indoor plants? Got a black thumb?

Try de-chlorinating your tap water by leaving it out on the counter for 24 hours,
And set it outside on a full moon to collect metaphysical energy!
Your snake plant will bless you with abundance and prosperity! Or, at the very least, it should stay alive.

Hint:
Put me
in your
Wealth or
Fame gua!

Follow emilypaper.com for more information!

Coming soon from Emmy Tidning

Sloane's Solitude

EMMY TIDNING

Sloane's Solitude

A second sight mystery

Sloane has no special powers, zero magical insights, and a mental illness that keeps her homebound. When a body is discovered and her hot new neighbor is involved, will she run, or be the next victim?

Seclude yourself with *Sloane's Solitude*, 2023

Made in the USA
Las Vegas, NV
24 October 2023

79666805R00142